SICK OBSESSION
THE TORTURED SOULS

KINSLEY KINCAID

Copyright © 2024 by Kinsley Kincaid

All rights reserved.

No part of this book may be reproduced in any form or by any electronic or mechanical means, including information storage and retrieval systems, without written permission from the author, except for the use of brief quotations in a book review.

ISBN eBook: 978-1-0688482-4-7

ISBN Paperback: 978-1-0688482-5-4

ISBN Omnibus Hardcover: 978-1-998646-13-5

Editing: Daisie Mae - Editing & Proofreading

Proofreading: The Cauldron Author Services

Cover Design: Ghoulie Graphics

NOTE FROM THE AUTHOR

Please be aware this book contains many **dark themes** and subjects that may be uncomfortable/unsuitable for some readers. This book contains **heavy themes** throughout. Please keep this in mind when entering ***Sick Obsession***. Content warnings are listed on authors' social pages & website.

This book and its contents are entirely a work of fiction. Any resemblance or similarities to names, characters, organizations, places, events, incidents, or real people are entirely coincidental or used fictitiously.

If you find any genuine errors, please reach out to the author directly to correct it. Thank you.

This book is intended for 18+ only.

If you or someone you know is in need of help or assistance text 988 or go to findahelpline.com

I believe you.

PLAYLIST

Behind Blue Eyes - Limp Bizkit
My tears ricochet - Taylor Swift
Superman's Dead - Our Lady Peace
Bullet With Butterfly Wings - The Smashing Pumpkins
Never Ever - All Saints
LosT - Bring Me The Horizon
Going Under - Evanescence
I Caught Fire - The Used
Dirty Little Secret - The All-American Rejects
Blue and Yellow - The Used
twin flame - mgk
Fighter - Christina Anguilera
This Is What It Feels Like - Amin van Buuren, Trevor Guthrie
Afterglow - Taylor Swift

DEX

BEFORE SUTTON

Raindrops ricochet against the thin glass window. My brain goes tick-tock with each tap. Lightning ignites the room with light, which is followed by an earth-shaking drum of thunder. Pieces of my dark hair rest upon my forehead as I lay in my bed, under the covers, fully clothed.

Tick Tock.

This will be the last night this happens. My body trembles as vivid memories flash through my memory. Shaking my head, squeezing my eyes closed, *shut up, shut up.*

As the memories disappear, the visions fade to black.

Suppressing is easier than reliving it.

Each night, I relive the last memory. Her tiny hands

caressing my arm. The soft voice whispering, coaxing me, "You love this part, don't you, Dex?"

No.

Shut up, Shut up.

A creak outside my door freezes my body. Eyes snap open.

Tick Tock.

All breathing is stopped, and eyes are focused on the thin opening between my door and the floor.

Another creak, this one louder, causes my lip to tremble.

Soon the dim glint of light that exposed the thin opening is disturbed. The brass door knob jingles slightly as it is touched.

Tick Tock.

The latch clicks, and the door is slowly pushed open.

My room is near my parents' room. The subtle movements are deliberate.

A racing heart beats against my chest. Her petite frame slides in quickly, wearing a thin nightgown down to her knees; the neckline is modest, with bare feet exposed. Long sandy blonde hair flows over her shoulders, and her silhouette casts against the white door as she closes it.

Lightning flashes through my window once again, exposing my guest.

My sister.

Her eyes focus on me as her lips smirk into a smile.

She is excited.

My face and body, for that matter, do not react. We will not react.

As the lightning fades, the crack of thunder vibrates once more. She gets closer. My legs shake as my mouth goes dry.

My bed is pushed against the wall. There is only one way for her to slide in. As she stands beside me, her mouth whispers, "Hi Dex."

You are not welcome here, is what I want to say, but I cannot force the words to leave my lips.

Brushing her hand over my blankets, she finds the corner of the soft fabric covering my body. Edging it open, inch by inch, as time slows.

The blanket begins to expose my arm; my fingers twitch, rubbing the nylon between them. A chill washes over me as I become more exposed. Her knee lifts to the bed as the blanket continues to move. Adrenaline courses through my veins.

She leans forward to move more of her body onto the bed.

Then everything happens too fast.

Gripping her wrist with one hand, I leave the nylon rope next to me as I reach for her ankle, which is hanging off the edge.

A tiny yelp leaves her as she is caught off guard.

Sitting up, I pull her onto the bed, bending her so I can grip her wrist and ankle using just my one hand. She is tiny compared to my larger frame.

"Dex, what are you doing?" Her words are spoken with venom and rage.

Grabbing the rope, I begin to tie her. Her free hand tries to stop me, but it doesn't work.

Scratch me, hit me, punch me.

I'll take it over and over again if it means tonight is the last night.

Not focusing on the pain caused by her actions any longer, I focus on finishing this tie. I've been preparing for days. Running it over and over again in my head.

I will not fail.

Once I have the rope secure around her one ankle and wrist, I pull her closer, twisting her around so her free limbs are near me. Reaching out, I grip each of them tightly, which causes her to whimper.

"You're hurting me. Stop!"

The demand is not one I will entertain.

She never stopped.

She always fucking hurt me!

Wrapping the rest of the nylon rope around her other wrist and then ankle, I loop it a couple times before knotting it off.

She is now hog-tied and defenseless.

Her back arches as she squirms, trying to pull free while laying stuck on her stomach.

I will not say *her* name. She will not get any power here tonight or ever again.

Maneuvering around her, I slide off the bed first.

Gripping the rope, I pull her tiny frame up and allow

her to hang for a moment. Hoping she is absorbing every moment of this, just as I did night after night.

Placing her gently to the floor, to not cause a commotion, I reach into my pocket and pull out a sock.

"Let me the fuck go, now, Dex!"

Bending down, as my name leaves her lips for the last time, I shove the sock inside her mouth. Silencing her.

Gripping the thin, delicate fabric of her nightgown, I tear it open, exposing her pale skin.

She is bare underneath.

As I let go of the fabric, it drapes on the ground, on either side of her.

Walking to my ensuite bathroom, I find my razor and smash it apart. The plastic breaks, and the five small blades are exposed.

The pain she will feel will never replace what I have felt.

But if this can make her feel just an ounce of it, this will all be worth it.

Taking all five into my hand, I step back into my room. The cool metal against my fingers sends a tingling sensation throughout my body.

Looking down, my sister is still trying to wiggle out of my hogtie. A waste of effort, I used a constrictor knot; it's the tightest and most secure knot. The more she pulls, the tighter it gets.

Placing one leg on the other side of her, I squat down and sit on her bottom. A muffled moan leaves her; surely the weight of me hurts her tiny bones.

Gripping her hair, I expose her bare neck.

This is where I will start.

Dropping all the blades next to me with the exception of one, I place the edge against the base of her skull where it meets her soft neck.

Slicing her skin, my fingers flood with her warm blood. Moving the blade, while keeping it angled, I move from the center of her neck and work my way around her skull, following her hairline the best I can. Her forehead is pressed against the floor as I reach just behind her ear and stop so I can complete the other side. Wild sobs are muffled, but I tune them out. My focus is clear. With each slice, relief and satisfaction radiate off me.

As I reach her other ear, I drop the blade.

Gripping her skin, my fingers force their way underneath. The blood makes it slippery and harder to grip, but it does not stop me. With all the force I can muster , I pull the skin up towards the crown of her head. It does not peel as I thought it would, easily. Squeezing it as hard as I can, a grunt leaves me as I force it more. My muscles and core activate; loud tears can be heard, but the sounds seem so far away from where I am. As more skin from her scalp pulls up, I am able to get a much better grip and reduce my efforts.

Her skin rips and tears the more I pull. Removing it from its home, her body, her muscles and her bones.

It takes some time, but I finally make it to where her forehead is resting on the ground. Picking up the blade, I slice the overhanging skin off her, tossing it next to us.

Admiring my work, I move my blade back to her neck. This time tilting it down along the already cut edge, giving my fingers room to grip under the bloodied skin.

My eyes are fascinated as my mind and body react with pleasure.

Blood is running down my arms. As my ears have become numb to her whimpers of distress and excessive movements, which were once loud as she tried to escape me.

This is my moment.

I finally feel free.

Time is not something I have thought of the entire time.

The precise, delicate movements of my hands and blade have me captivated. Pulling the last piece of skin off my sister's face, which I saved for last, I toss it next to the rest of it on the floor. At some point, she died.

I couldn't tell you when. I was too entranced by my work before me.

My body is covered in her.

Images begin to flash before my eyes yet again.

No, no, no. Shut up, shut up.

My blade drops to the ground; I used all five. As they got dull, I replaced it with a new one.

Racing to my bathroom, I jump in the bathtub.

Gripping my hair with my hands, I pull it hard.

Suppress, motherfucker!

The back of my head hits the tiled wall behind me. Cracking as it connects.

My body rocks back and forth. Blood pools around me.

Her hands on my skin. Her body fluids on my leg, as she used me. Caressing my manhood while panting in my ear.

A monstrous roar jumps out of me.

Loud screams can be heard. High-pitched screams of terror.

My body still rocks in place.

The light turns on.

"Dex. What did you do?"

Frozen, I cannot respond to my mother, who is hysterical before me.

"I called 911."

My father's deep voice invades me.

It's too late, can't they see? She is already dead.

No one can save her.

Just like no one saved me.

CHAPTER 1
DEX

AFTER SUTTON

Sitting in the treeline, even sheltered by the shade of overhanging branches, the hot summer heat here in Georgia engulfs me. Sweat drips off the tip of my nose onto my lips. Each time I lick them, the delicious salty flavor satisfies my tastebuds. My short hair is hidden by the hood of my black sweater. Regardless of the heat, I always wear it. As more time passes, the heavier it gets, soaking with my sweat and sticking to my body.

My legs are clad in cut-off black jeans, just above the knee, with a pair of black skate shoes on my feet. Deep down, I hope for a short cool breeze to brush past me; it has yet to come. It's nearly ninety degrees. Everything feels sticky and muggy, and it's possible that I am melting and don't even realize it.

Leaning my head back against the large tree behind me, my eyes are heavy. At any moment, they may close and not reopen. Dehydration mixed with heat stroke. None of that matters, because I never miss a day. Since the first day I saw this rare creature, I have spent hours upon hours out here, sitting, waiting and watching.

Not once has this majestic soul noticed me lurking in the shadows; perhaps she has, but has never brought attention to it. I am here from after sunrise to nightfall. Never wanting to miss my moment alone with her. Some days I have chores and errands. I race to get them done without being noticeable before sneaking away. Mama knows I like my alone time, exploring our new home while keeping close, just in case.

On days where I can't be here the entire time, it's hit or miss. She never presents herself at the same time each day; it is always a guessing game, a wait and see.

Today, I have been here since sunrise. It's noon. The sun continues to get warmer, and my body begs for me to remove my sweater, but I won't, not ever.

It helps keep me safe.

Terrible things happen when I am exposed and isolated.

Shaking my head, squeezing my eyes shut, *shut up, shut up*, I repeat until all the intrusive thoughts that are trying to invade my memory are back where they belong. In the vault deep within my brain. Closed shut and locked away, until they escape again.

My eyes are fading; sweat builds on my eyebrows.

Beads of it begin to slide down my eyelids onto my lashes. Blinking, a drop slips into my eyes. The salt stings. I use my sleeve to rub the rest of my sweat off as my eyes water. Instinct wants me to squeeze my eyes shut until it stops, but logic tells me to keep blinking it out. As I go with logic, blinking rapidly, an object appears before me. Squinting, until the fog in my vision dissipates, they are holding a basket standing in the meadow surrounded by wildflowers. Beautiful red hair, which is tied back into a braid today, hangs down her mid back. A white summer dress decorated with daisies drapes over her pale skin. She never wears shoes. Today is no different with her feet bare. A large sun hat is on top of her head as her tiny fingers begin to collect today's fresh flowers. A mix of purple, white, and blue pop against her brown woven hand basket. Beautiful hums join in with the chirping of birds. She is the most majestic creature I've ever seen.

My eyes move up her bare arms, with the sun beating down. I hope she remembered sunscreen; I would hate for her to burn.

Her head turns, highlighting her profile; long lashes curled and her nose is like a button. My heartbeat is in my ears, and my palms have become even more sweaty, as I hope she doesn't turn further around and see me.

Teeth bite her lower lip as her hand reaches out, pulling on a cluster of yellow buttercups to add to the collection. At the same time, a dominant, deep male voice echoes through the woods, "Izzie, let's go."

Izzie, moving my lips, I repeat it to myself, Izzie.

I've never heard her name before. And to have it enter my ear and tickle my lips brings warmth inside of me. As I am focusing on her name, Izzie. I hear a sigh of frustration leaving her as she moves to face the direction of the unknown voice. Her body changes; she is annoyed as she starts to leave me behind. A breeze blows past us out of nowhere, and her dress hem flows around her, as I close my eyes. I let cool air wash over me, and I swear I can smell her sweet scent mixed with florals. As I reopen my eyes, I move them back to where she is, or was.

She's gone. I've just learnt her name, and she is gone. Our time was cut short; usually she pitters in the meadows for what feels like hours, perhaps only in my mind. It may only be mere minutes. Letting out a breath of frustration, my head falls against the tree. I just wanted a little more time with her. He ruined it. He took her from me too soon.

Anger builds in my chest; my arms tighten with tension as my fists ball. Rising to my feet, twigs crunch under them as I begin my walk back home to mama. I need my mama to help calm me.

I just wanted my time with her. I've waited here for fucking hours to see her. If she didn't show, it would be one thing, but she did. And I just wanted my time.

My fist hits a tree as I walk past; a short-lived tingle penetrates my bones. It doesn't help; my chest still heaves in frustration. More sweat covers me; even my legs are glistening and my socks are soaked inside of my shoes.

My breath heaves and my nostrils flare as fallen leaves crunch beneath each one of my steps.

Ducking under overhanging branches, the old barn, *home*, comes into sight. Mama. Safety. Stepping out of the shadows of the woods, I am in the clearing as mama jumps out from around the corner, startling me.

Sweat continues dripping down my face as I take in her disheveled dark hair as she fixes her top and adjusts her shorts. Jasper then pops out from the other side of the barn, holding his fist to his mouth as he coughs, leaning against the wall. I side-eye both of them, knowing exactly what I just interrupted.

"Dexy, you're back early." Mama rushes over, wrapping her arm around mine. "How was your walk?" Her eyes look up at me wide with unconditional love and genuine curiosity. She would never make me feel bad for interrupting. I shake my head once, communicating that I am not happy.

She squeezes my arm harder while speaking softly, "Let's get you inside, sweet boy. Jasp, will you get me a cool cloth?"

Almost immediately, I feel calmer. Mama never lets anything bad happen to me. She will always protect me.

Walking slowly up to the old barn doors, I close my eyes and breathe in once more, which helps clear my head.

Jasper slides the large wooden barn door open, and we follow. The space is open; we have redone it over our time here. The main level houses a kitchen against one wall, with a table, couch and television off to the other. We even fitted an indoor bathroom so mama could have her own private toilet and shower. Jasper and I can do our business anywhere, and I don't mind using the hose to shower. The cool water feels good against my skin on hot days, but I only use it in the dark under the moonlight.

A set of wooden stairs goes to the loft area above; we built a wall in the middle to give us our own spaces. I have my room, and they share the other.

It took us time to gather everything we needed to turn the barn into our home, but we did, and I hope we never have to leave it.

Mama leads us to the couch; once we reach it, she sits first and then pulls me down next to her. My head falls over to her shoulder, and my body cuddles in closer. Her hand cups my cheek as she whispers words of reassurance, "It's ok, mama's here. I got you. I always will, Dexy. Breathe for me, please, my sweet boy."

Nodding in response, I whisper, "Mama." As I relax further into her.

She is only gentle like this with me and sometimes Jasper. If you aren't us, then I would hate to be you.

My mama is Iris Ashford. Her twin brother and twin flame is Jasper Ashford. They are the infamous Ashford Twins, who mutilated and murdered their parents at the age of fifteen. They took me in once I arrived in Sutton. The three of us were always supposed to be. And together, we slaughtered and then burnt down Sutton

Asylum while releasing several of its patients back into society.

Dangerous and deranged. Some would say. But to me, to us, we are family.

A cool cloth replaces her soft hand against my warm skin. It feels fantastic. My eyes fade, and I give into the exhaustion. Until tomorrow, Izzie.

CHAPTER 2
DEX

A few days have passed.

After giving into my exhaustion, I woke up in my bed the next morning, still fully dressed. Jasp must have carried me up.

We are family. I love my fucking family. I'm not blood; I didn't grow up with them, but we have chosen one another. My chosen family holds more significance to me than the one I was born into. They never protected me; they never tried to stop it and save me.

They are cowards.

Shut up, shut up.

I grip my hair while shaking my head. Squeezing my eyes shut, I let out a monstrous roar from deep within my chest.

No one's home to hear me.

They will never compare to what I have now.

Mama and Jasper.

And if those two ever stumbled upon my parents, I would sit back and enjoy the fucking show.

The flashing images of my past fade as new ones become prominent.

My parents tied up, gagged, and ready for our taking.

I would start by using a thin, sharp pin and slowly push multiple punctures into the whites of each of their eyes. Watching the tip as it disappears inside of them. Fascinated. Wondering if blood would follow or clear eye fluid.

Perhaps I would try and use the sharp tip of the pin to assist me in peeling back a layer as well. Meticulous tasks fascinate me.

Then, using the same pin, I would poke it through their nostrils and septum, leaving it there, limiting their airway with the obstruction.

Letting out a deep breath, I stop before getting carried away. I've been lost in these thoughts before; they last hours as I meticulously daydream each fucking detail.

Looking up at the wood-paneled ceiling, I should go back to the meadow.

I haven't since that day.

Izzie.

My beautiful Izzie.

Pushing my dark hair off my forehead, I get up off my bed and head downstairs, grabbing my sweater on the way out. Pulling the barn door open, the hot sun immediately shines on me, and the humidity attaches itself to me.

Does it ever rain in this fucking place?

Stepping out, I look around. No sign of mama or Jasp as I close the door behind me. Flipping my hood over my head, I make my way through the shaded woods. Ducking under the low-hanging branches, I know my way to the meadow like the back of my hand. But I never take the same way twice. It's too easy to make a trail, and I can't have people finding a worn path, then finding us.

We are wanted, nation-wide.

I wouldn't doubt there is also a large price tag over our heads if found and delivered back to the state of North Carolina.

We slaughtered Sutton Asylum, then burnt it down.

Comes with the territory.

Sun is starting to break through ahead of me. The meadow presents itself to me and the beauty within.

She's here.

Hair flowing behind her as she skips filling her basket with fresh wildflowers.

Always in her sunhat and pretty dresses, her energy is carefree and happy. I wonder what that's like.

I am happy; I love the life I have now, but you can see her life hasn't been tainted by evil. Evil like me.

Sitting down against the trunk of a large tree, I watch and admire.

Once her basket is full, she gracefully sits down on the lush green grass; her profile is toward me. I have all her curves and ridges memorized, but each time I see them, it's like it's the first time all over again.

A rustle comes from behind me. I don't move; she does.

I freeze. Her eyes appear to be staring directly at me.

Fuck, please don't see me.

Izzie's brows furrow as she squints, trying to gauge the sound. Moments pass; we don't hear the sound again, so she turns back around.

Blowing out a sigh of relief, fuck. It's never been that close before, to her seeing me. I don't know what I would have done if she saw me and approached me. Most likely, I would have ran away, but who fucking knows.

Taking my hand, I rub it across my face, removing the excess sweat that continuously drips down my body.

Izzie stands, bending over to grip her woven basket, and begins to walk away. As she walks away, her head turns back, analyzing the space she's left behind and the treeline around her. Before fully disappearing, she focuses forward again and skips off.

I remain seated.

I've never followed her. I've never explored where her path has gone. Temptation has toyed with my mind, but thus far, I have been able to resist. But since the other day, when she was taken from me before our time was up, it's been running through my head more. What if it happens again? If I could only see where she goes, maybe we can have more time?

I would never fucking hurt her.

Izzie calms me. She holds a life I could only dream of having.

She is free.

It was still early in the day when she left.

I went into town and got groceries, which were paid for in cash. We live near a small, quiet town; curious minds usually stare and watch me while I make my way through the town center and pick up our things. Some have tried to talk to me; I acknowledge them, but I do not speak. I've built a rapport with few; if they see me they say hello, and I nod in return, which makes them smile. I'm not sure where they think I came from; perhaps they have seen me on the news. Maybe they think I am alone, without the Ashfords, and leave me be?

Like the meadow, I never take the same route home.

I won't be the reason my family is risked or separated.

I'm back home now, roaming outside when I hear, "Dexy, come here."

It's mama.

Walking back towards the barn, I see her and Jasp standing outside with big grins on their faces. I'm suspicious.

Mama runs up to me, she is electric. "We have a surprise!" Jasp shakes his head chuckling, while opening the large barn door. "This was all you, Savage."

Gripping my hand, mama leads me inside and Jasp follows. We walk, rushed to the cold storage door at the back of the barn. Mama has let go of me, now bouncing on the balls of her feet while her hands cover her mouth while she giggles.

Since we have a fridge now, we don't use the cold storage anymore, so what is she so excited over?

"I'm so fucking excited!" Her voice goes high pitched as Jasp bends down to lift the latch. As he does, mama jumps while pointing toward the hole now exposed and yells, "SURPRISE!"

Taken aback, I look at her confused. What is she talking about?

Stepping forward, I look down as my eyes take in the dark space below. I gasp in shock and disbelief.

Bright green eyes are looking back at me.

It's her.

CHAPTER 3
IZZIE

My teeth are chattering with my body balled up into myself.

I hate wearing shoes; I love feeling the earth beneath my feet, it grounds me. I've always been a country girl.

But today, I wish I had worn them. Sharp, jagged rocks are stabbing the pads of my feet, no matter where I place them. Although, at this point, I can barely feel anything. It's freezing here.

My nose drips; no matter how much I sniffle it back, it's of no use. Goosebumps must be decorating me. I'm only in my sundress, and when I was thrown into this cold, damp hole, they gave me nothing else. My body shivers, battling the cold, trying to keep my internal temperature up. Closing my eyes, I let out a sigh.

I was caught off guard on my way home. It all happened so fast, I didn't even hear anyone behind me.

Strong hands covered my mouth. Smaller ones held my wrists, which were later bound together. I kicked back, but it did nothing; they were expecting it. My ankle was grabbed immediately. Once they had it, I knew I was fucked.

They had me.

As I was being carried away, my basket full of wildflowers remained behind, disheveled, along the path home.

My brother will come looking. I don't know what time it is, but I know I'm late. He will see my flowers and know. He will know the fucking Ashfords have taken me.

They think we don't know.

We do.

One day we came home to our rooms ransacked and clothes missing. It was after the big fire at the infamous Sutton Asylum, where many patients and staff ended up dead, captured, or still at large. That night we went hunting. My brother, Liam and I thought they fled until we found the abandoned barn. It would be the perfect place to hide, surrounded by woods with no foot traffic.

Sliding the door just an inch, the moonlight shone inside. That's when we saw them, sleeping on a pile of old hay with our shit next to them.

That night we made an unspoken truce. We would let *this* slide, just once.

But after that night, they better keep their distance and we would keep ours. Since then, Liam has put surveillance around our property, just to be sure.

I hope they captured this. My brother will be here any time, ready to blow this bitch up.

Until then, I wait. I sit in this freezing, dark hole, counting the minutes until I am out of here.

My thoughts are interrupted when I hear loud footsteps above me, followed by muffled voices. It's them, but there are more than just them. Curious.

I can hear the latch on the door squeak as it is raised; bright natural light shines down, which hurts my eyes initially.

"SURPRISE!" echoes in my ears as I see Iris's hands pointing down upon me.

The additional set of feet steps forward, dark hair hangs off his forehead, and he is wearing a black sweater with his hands in his pockets. As he takes me in, I do the same.

How has he not had a heat stroke wearing that?

A gasp leaves him; his eyes never leave mine.

His face is beautiful with thin lips and soft, dark eyes with those stunning long lashes all men seem to have. Defined cheekbones are chiseled onto his face.

"Do you like it?" Iris giggles in excitement while clapping her hands together. Then it occurs to me, I know exactly who this third person is. I did research after we found them at night months ago; she had a pet, an adopted son who arrived in Sutton years after their sentence. He is just as dangerous when he wants to be.

It's Dex.

DEX

Her eyes haven't left mine. She isn't scared, but her body trembles. Natural light catches her arms, which brings attention to the blonde pricked hair standing on them.

She's cold.

Stepping back, I throw my sweater over my head and drop it down to her. It lands just beside her in the small space, but she doesn't move. Rather freeze than take something from me.

My chest swells in disappointment. *Sweet Izzie, please let me help you.*

"You bitch. He gave you his sweater, put it on!" Mama shouts down, her anger echoes in the small hole below. Izzie flinches; if you were to blink, you would have missed it.

She continues sitting in defiance, not budging.

But her lips part, smiling back, "Once my brother gets here, you are so fucked."

Izzie's voice is captivating. Soft, but confident.

Iris starts laughing hysterically. "We are going to have so much fun with you." Ignoring Izzie's claims completely.

Jasper steps around; his hand is wrapping around her throat, their matching tattoos on display, *yours* and *mine.*

"Savage, let's go have some of our own fun. Let Dex enjoy his present." His voice is low as he whispers seductively at mama. Her body instantly reacts to his; her pelvis grinds against his, teasing. Sticking her tongue out, she licks his cheek slowly before her lips move against his skin, "Fuck me, daddy, Jasp. I need your cock in my ass, now." Her lashes flutter, tickling him as he smirks.

Mama's eyes glance towards me. "We will leave you two alone, so you can get to know each other." Pausing, her chest starts to heave, "And if she tries anything, my sweet boy, you tell mama. I'll call upon the good doc, RIP, to help us in an impromptu session! He can help us decide how to punish a very bad girl, can't we? Although, with how we left him, he may not be much help." Mama's finger taps her chin as she ponders. Shrugging her shoulders, "Oh well. Let's go, Jasp. Dexy, have fun on your playdate."

Gripping Jasper's hand, she leads him skipping out of the barn.

Izzie's focus has remained unchanged; it's still on me. Then it occurs to me, I've left myself exposed. What was I thinking?

My fingers brush through my thick, dark hair, gripping it tightly as I pull. I need my sweater back. I need to be safe.

My body moves before I can think; my feet are rushing down the narrow stone steps. As I reach the last one, I sit and extend my hand forward quickly to get my sweater back. Then her tiny hand goes on top of mine, and my heart begins to race even faster as it drops into the pit of my stomach.

No.

Don't fucking touch me. She can't.

A loud growl erupts from me, which shocks her as she pulls back. Putting my sweater back on, I brush off the dirt that has attached to it and begin shaking. No one touches me.

Throwing my hood over my head, I squeeze my eyes shut. Memories flash vividly before me.

My sister's hand tracing circles on mine as her leg rubbed along my thigh. Lips kissing down my neck as I stayed still, hoping it would be quick this time.

Shut up, shut up.

My fist clenches as it shoots out, punching the hard rock wall next to me. It hurts, but with each punch, the images begin to fade. I can't stop until they are all gone. Once the feeling of her is gone, I stop. My eyes open. Looking down at my hand, my knuckles are battered and bloodied. Fingers are swelling as tingles radiate through my bones.

"I'm sorry." Her voice penetrates my focus. Looking towards her, she remains unmoved and unphased by the situation, yet she is apologizing. Why?

Moving my gaze to my feet, I shake my head briskly.

"I'm Izzie, what's your name?" She asks. I don't respond. Moments pass, the silence is comforting, yet she breaks it.

"Dexy, is it?"

My body moves up a step, only mama calls me that.

Her voice is rushed now, "Dex. Sorry, I meant Dex." I nod quickly in response but still keep my distance.

"Dex, will you help me? Will you let me go, please?"

Her tone has changed; it's more angelic now. But I'm not a moron. I know what she's trying to do. She thinks I'm weak, stupid, and naive. I'm anything but.

Looking up, I take her in once more, absolutely perfect. But I know she's playing me.

Standing up, I carefully turn on the narrow steps and go back up to the main floor. Panic hits her, "No Dex. Please. Don't leave me down here."

I slip my finger through the metal latch and close the cold storage door shut.

This is exactly what Doc would recommend. Sneaky, bad girls must be punished. It's the only way she will learn not to try it again.

CHAPTER 4
DEX

It's the next day. Mama and Jasper came back later that night. They left me be, not coming into my room to check on me.

Laying in bed, I was still awake, trying to sort everything out in my head. She's here. Within arm's reach, and I can't get near her without feeling pain and anguish rushing through my veins and prickling my skin.

This isn't fair.

Tears well in my eyes. Fuck.

My past will not define me. My past will not define me.

She's gone. I took care of it. Yet her touch still haunts me. Her breath still dances like the devil on my face.

Exhausted from the day, I eventually faded away. My sleep was restless. I woke up early in the quiet barn. I grab a banana from where I am in the kitchen and begin walking to where Izzie is being held.

Opening the cold storage door, I peek down and see her laying on her side, still curled up into herself, sleeping. Her beautiful, long red hair is fanned around her.

I make my way to the bottom step and sit, watching her. Her breathing is shallow as I study the rising of her chest. She must feel me because it only takes a few minutes before she awakens. With heavy eyes, she looks over to see me.

I place the banana on the ground before me and push it forward. She doesn't resist, grabbing the fruit quickly, then begins to peel it. As she takes each bite, I continue to study her. I don't feel threatened by her, but I also don't feel fully comfortable. I'm confused, not completely sure how to be in this situation yet.

What I do know is that my sweater will keep me safe.

Bending over, I brush my finger in the dirt and spell my name: Dex. She watches me meticulously. Once she realizes what I am doing, my name slips from her lips, and her voice is hoarse. Hitting my head with my sore hand, I am so fucking stupid. She needs water; what was I thinking?

"No. It's ok. Please, don't hurt yourself." Izzie pleads.

I'm feeling overwhelmed and unsure.

This is different from the woods. She couldn't see or speak to me. I could watch her peacefully without fear or worry for hours. But now, being able to smell her sweet scent and hear her soft voice, I'm disoriented, my mind is moving a mile a minute, and I am trying to sort through all the chaos of it.

Mustering up all the courage I have, I stop hitting myself and run back up the stairs and get her a bottle of water. I remove the cap, then go back down. It's warm, but it should be fine. I set it down on the ground and push it slightly forward towards her.

"I won't hurt you, I promise. And I'm sorry for yesterday, that was stupid. I know you're smarter than to let me charm you into releasing me. I should have known better." She apologizes before taking a sip from the bottle.

It doesn't matter.

As unsettled as I am to have her here, this close. She isn't leaving me. Mama gave me a gift, and I am keeping it. I decided this last night, while laying in bed.

I'll take her for walks to the meadow whenever she wants. We can decorate her space and find her all the sundresses she wants. But I am keeping her.

Then a loud bang startles me.

Izzie's eyes widen as the largest grin comes across her face.

"Open this motherfucking door, you psychotic fucks! I am here for my sister."

No, no, no.

I just got her.

Footsteps rush down the stairs above me. Mama and Jasper as they rush to the door.

"So fucked now that my brother's here." Izzie whispers.

Manipulator.

Just like my sister, but in a different way. I think.

I can't trust her, but my curiosity has heightened. A majestic beauty who spends hours in the meadow, has so much more to her behind those beautiful green eyes and flowy dresses.

The door slides open, and a deep voice fills the space, "Give her back to me. NOW!" It's the same voice that stole her from me that day.

He is here to do it again.

No, no, no.

"Liam!" Izzie shouts.

My hands cover my ears, and my eyes squeeze shut as my body rocks.

"We found her. We are keeping her. She is our pet now." Mama's voice is firm, but it doesn't matter. I can feel a breeze as the pads of Izzie's feet race past me.

"I know you watch my sister, you sick fuck. We have cameras all over those woods." His voice is back.

No, make it stop.

Commotion starts behind me. But I remain seated, shaking, hoping for it all to stop.

I don't know how much time passes when a hand touches my shoulder.

I jump, my body reacts; *don't touch me.*

"Dexy, it's me." I lean into mama's touch, feeling comforted.

"I'm sorry, sweet boy, she's gone. She bolted out the first chance she got. I'm so sorry. It was supposed to be a present for you. I saw how much you wanted her." Shaking my head, I whisper, "It's okay, mama."

"Dex, buddy, maybe we should stay away from the meadow for a bit? Just to be safe?" Jasp suggests. I nod understanding; we don't know these people, they could tell someone we are here. A single tear runs down my cheek.

I'm overwhelmed by this entire experience. Unable to process it all quick enough.

Fuck.

Lips kiss the top of my head, "I'm sorry, my sweet boy."

CHAPTER 5
IZZIE

Stepping out of the shower, I look at the fogged mirror and see 'MINE' freshly written on it.

He was in here, and I didn't even know. He could have done anything he wanted. But he did this. Reminding me who I belong to after an unexpected night away.

Water droplets run down each letter as I bite down on my bottom lips. My nipples perk, "His," leaves me as I whisper to myself.

The bathroom is small; it only takes a few steps on the cool tile to make it from the dual bathtub shower to the sink and mirror. Reaching my hand up, I wipe more of the mirror off, exposing more of my reflection. Damp red hair hangs over my shoulders, dripping down my pale skin decorated with millions of tiny freckles. My green eyes stare back at me as I continue to take myself in.

I don't grab a towel. The hot Georgia heat mixed

with the humidity is overwhelming; the last thing I want is to be cuddled in a towel. Perspiration lingers on my fingertips as I touch the gap between my breasts and begin delicately moving them down my body. Watching myself in the reflection, my breath hitches as I reach my bare pelvic area. With my middle finger, I draw circles on my sensitive skin. Goosebumps raise as a shiver rushes through me.

At the same time, I hear the squeak of the bathroom door opening.

Liam.

I don't stop.

"Move lower." He demands. I keep my eyes on my reflection as my finger inches down, then disappears between my swollen lips; I'm wet.

"Now suck. Taste yourself."

A smirk forms across my face. Using the palm of my hand, I grind my clit against it, disobeying my brother. Electric shocks radiate through me; it feels so fucking good. My hips buck as I stick three fingers inside of me; finding my g-spot, I continue to work myself.

I'm panting, chasing the release I so deeply desire.

Liam doesn't stop me for not listening. From the corner of my eye, I can see him watching, arms crossed over his chest.

He is in black skinny jeans and a white crop top, which he made himself out of an old tee. His body is covered in ink, which is a drastic contrast to his bright white hair. Which is his natural hair color, believe it or not.

Liam can tell I am watching him; a sinister smile forms, showcasing his sharp teeth as he growls at me through them.

My legs tremble as I work myself harder. Returning my focus back on my reflection, my face is flushed as the orgasm builds.

"Fuck." Is the only word I can get out as my release takes over. My pussy is pulsating around my fingers; my clit swells the faster I grind, using myself. The familiar wave washes over me as cum coats my fingers. I don't let up, working myself through it, taking every drop I can. My legs want to give out, as my free hand reaches out to brace myself, holding the sink. The last wave hits as I slow my movements down and begin removing my fingers from inside my pussy. Cum glistens off them.

Moving my fingers up, I trace my lips, then open my mouth. One by one, I place my fingers between my lips and close down around them. Hollowing my cheeks, I suck, lapping my release clean off me. Seductively, I slowly pull my fingers out from between my pouty lips and let out a deep breath as my heart continues to race in my chest.

"May I have some more?" I ask innocently.

A hoarse chuckle fills the room, following my question, "What do you want this time?"

Gripping my nipples between both thumbs and forefingers, I squeeze, arching my back, "The meadow."

Liam walks behind me; his dark brown eyes look into mine. His arms wrap around me as he places his hands over mine, squeezing my fingers tighter around my nipples. It stings, as a harsh hiss leaves me as I arch into him, my ass pushes back, his hard cock can be felt under his rough black jeans. My head rests on his chest as my wet hair begins to curl into itself.

His teeth nip my ear, and his smirk remains unchanged as the firm "No." escapes him.

I whimper, my face pouts.

"Your fucking tricks work on everyone, except for me."

Grinding against him harder, I don't change the expression on my face, trying once more to get my way. On the way home from spending a lovely night in the Ashfords cold storage, he was clear. No meadow until he can ensure they have moved on from their fascination with us.

It's not the twins who are, it's Dex. I wasn't going to argue. Eventually, he will give in.

"No meadow. For now."

The 'for now' is new. My face stays neutral; if I celebrate the small win, he will take it back. Reading people is what I do. Playing them so I win comes easily to me.

"Don't clean up; I want you still dripping while sitting in your cute little sundress, eating the lunch I made you." Liam winks at me before quickly kissing my neck and leaving.

SICK OBSESSION

Speaking to myself, "Of course, brother, as you wish."

CHAPTER 6
DEX

Mama said no more meadow. That if she saw either of them again around me, she would take great pleasure in killing them slowly for ruining her gift. And that she didn't want anything to happen to me, in case I went back and the man was there, waiting.

It's been nine days, and my skin is itching. Crawling with discomfort and need. I need to see her. It's never been this fucking long.

Sitting on my bed with my back against the wall, my knees are curled into my chest as my arms are wrapped around my legs. My mind keeps chanting, *get up, get up, go.*

To disobey mama would be monumental; it's nothing I have done before. She protects me. I trust her.

Jasper went to town today to collect our essentials from the general store. Mama isn't home, I haven't heard her since Jasper left. Looking around my bare room, with hair hanging over my forehead, I brush it back as my heart races. My thumbnail picks at my other hand, just a peak wouldn't hurt. To make sure she is okay.

Rocking back and forth, conflict races through me. I'm not going to hurt her. I would never hurt her. If I ever scream, mama would come for me, she would help me.

It's a split-second decision.

Rotating my body, I let go of my legs as they fall over the side of my bed. My shoe-clad feet touch the floor as I rise. Grabbing my sweater, I pull it over my head and throw my hood up. It's another hot summer day, I always wear my armor.

Opening my door, I race down the wooden steps. My legs are moving. Mama could come back any moment and stop me. And I would let her.

As I reach the main level, my eyes scan the area as my mind bombards me with conflicting thoughts, the devil on one side and an angel on the other.

Shaking my head, I squeeze my eyes, and with a closed fist, I hit the side of my head, *shut up, shut up, shut up.*

This usually works. The voices fade as I open the sliding barn door. Opening my eyes, the bright sun invades the dark space, and the heat hits me immediately. It takes a moment to adjust as I continue moving quickly. Beelining it to the thick woods, twigs snap beneath my feet.

Then I stop. I'm being stupid. If she is there, I need to move carefully. I growl, angry at myself. This quick break has brought the voices back.

No. I'm doing this. Shut up!

I silently scream back to them.

My nostrils flare. I'm almost there, I will not let them win. I need to see Izzie.

Gingerly, I continue on. Strategically watching where my next step will be, clear of any twigs or crunchy leaves. My hands use the trees on either side of me to keep my balance as I tiptoe through the thick foliage.

This technique takes me longer. I may even miss seeing her. Though, at least I tried and gave into my cravings.

Reaching the treeline by the clearing, I find a large tree trunk to lean up against. I slide down slowly; my knees are bent, and I throw my arms over them and wait.

She isn't here. Unsure of the time, it's possible Izzie has already come. It is possible she has already picked her basket of fresh wild flowers while prancing barefoot in the long grass.

Then I think, what if she comes and spots me? What if she sees me and starts screaming because she is afraid of me?

I would never hurt her. I just want to see her.

Shaking my head quickly, the image disappears, but the anxiety builds.

My sweater is already glued to my body with sweat,

but it doesn't matter. It never fucking matters. She is always worth it.

Hours have passed. It's dark.

I've never stayed this late. If mama and Jasper are home, they either think I am still in my room or know exactly where I am. Disobeying.

Standing up, my legs are stiff as I kick them out in an effort to stretch. Stepping forward, my body leads me from being within the treeline to being outside of it, standing in the meadow. My eyes scan the area, this is all new to me. It's pitch dark; the moon and stars shine down, helping me see. It's uncomfortable. Being on this side, I prefer lingering in the shadows.

But I don't stop here; I keep moving. The desire for her will only continue until my cravings are fulfilled. I know where her house is. I won't get too close, perhaps just a glimpse will do?

Making my way through the shrubs, long grass, and trees located on the opposite side of the clearing, it should take me directly to her. A few branches get caught on my sweater, tugging it backwards before I snap them off.

A large two-story home begins to appear. Looking at all the windows that I can make out, it's dark inside.

What if her brother got angry at her? Hurt her?

What if she thinks we were going to hurt her?

She needs to know mama wouldn't have, I don't think. Izzie was a gift for me. I would have taken care of her, always.

Looking around, I don't find any noticeable surveillance cameras, which makes me more brave. Moving forward, my feet begin to take me towards the back door. My breathing is shallow, as I carefully move with my eyes remaining on high alert. Crickets are chirping, it's soothing and relaxing. Focusing on them, anxiety subsides, even if it's just for a moment. Because the minute I reach my hand out to touch the cool door handle, it rapidly invades my body again.

Swallowing, my hand shakes as I begin to turn it. It's unlocked. Nothing stops me from fully rotating the knob and pulling the door open. A tiny squeak comes from the hinge, my eyes widen as fear hits me. Staying still, I wait. Seconds feel like minutes. Still, no movement from within the house can be heard. I stay like this for a while longer to ensure they aren't doing the same thing to me, waiting for my next move.

Once satisfied that it is safe, I slip through the opening and close the door quietly behind me.

The moon shines through the window just enough to show me I am in the kitchen. My feet pad across the room, and just as I am about to explore the rest of the house, my nose catches a distinct foul odor. My palms sweat, and a clear image of that night flashes before me as I sat in the bathtub rocking, as *she* was in the other room left to bleed out and rot.

Then it occurs to me. It could be her.

It could be Izzie.

Following the scent, I continue to move. I am hyper-focused on it, no longer paying attention to anything else around me.

The trail leads directly to the fridge. With trembling hands, I wrap my fingers around the handle and pull it open. A bright light comes on from within. My breath hitches as I take in the sight before me. The interior is stark white, the shelves are matching but made of racking. Two large, clear containers sit at the base as something from above drips into them. My gaze moves, following each drop. Tilting my head to the side, I take in the sight before me. The odor becomes less noticeable the longer I stand here.

Two sets of eyes are looking back at me. One from a male, which are brown, and the other from a female, which are green. I focus on the green eyes. No shine, no sparkle left. The soul has faded, and lifelessness remains. Short, curly gray hair sits on her head, and the male head is bald. A sigh of relief escapes my body, neither are Izzie.

I continue to take this in. Both mouths have settled into a frown as their skin droops towards the clean cut at the neck. This wasn't a quick, careless job, this was planned and perfectly executed. I get lost in admiring the work and wondering what the containers of blood would be for?

"Dex Ashford, formally Dex Ryan, who was also formally Dexter John Walters. Born on October 7th to two drug addict parents. Later sold at the age of ten to the Ryan family, who you may know as mom and dad, for drug money. And the sole purpose of the Ryan's acquiring you... drum roll, please." He pauses for effect, "So their daughter wouldn't get handsy with their biological son. Your brother. Early signs of her tendencies warned them. Apparently, she was getting a little too handsy. So, they got you for *her*. What a gift. *Her* own personal toy," A deep, angry voice states from behind me.

My eyes shift, and I can hear my heart racing in my ears. I turn around slowly, closing the fridge as I move. The kitchen light is on as I take in everything around me.

Decorating the walls is white paint, possibly with words of all sizes scratched into it aggressively.

"Is that what my sister was for you? Is that why that crazy bitch tried to steal her from me?"

My eyes meet his; his hair is white, and he's wearing a crop tee and black tight jeans with ink covering his exposed skin. High-Top sneakers are on his feet, which are firmly planted to the linoleum flooring.

For years, *she* did vile things to me. Unspeakable disgusting things, and I just took it. I would never fucking do that to another person. My hand balls into a tight fist.

He remains unphased, casually standing before me.

Then my brain catches up to what he just said. He knew my name. He knows my birthday.

What does he mean I was sold?

"Liam! Stop. Leave him alone." A female voice can

faintly be heard as the room spins around me. Placing my hands over my ears, I fall to the ground, "Mama, mama, mama..."

Is all I say continuously, repeating myself. My body shakes, "Mama, mama, mama..."

A tiny hand applies pressure on my arm, and I scream loudly as I squeeze my eyes shut, still rocking and not letting up. My vocal cords begin to sting, but I can't stop. Everything goes black as the air from my lungs becomes desolate.

"Mama's here. I'm here, it's okay, sweet boy. Mama is here."

Her arms squeeze me, and I can feel her legs resting on either side of me. Her soft whispers of reassurance penetrate my ears, it helps calm me.

"What did those fucks do to him?" Mama clearly snarks.

Mama is pissed. They should be fucking terrified.

CHAPTER 7
DEX

A cool breeze traces delicately over my face as I rock back and forth. That's when I realized I'm no longer in *her* house. But I can feel mama; her tiny arms are still wrapped around me, keeping me safe. A deep voice interrupts the voices and thoughts in my head.

"Dexy, can you tell us what happened?"

It's Jasper.

I don't understand. How did I get outside? When did I get here?

Removing my hands from my head, I place them on the ground around me and feel cool, crisp grass under my fingertips. Slowly opening my eyes, they are met with darkness. Taking a deep breath in, the scent is familiar. I'm in the meadow.

"My sweet boy, it's ok." Mama continues to comfort

me as I calm down. I can still hear my heart beating rapidly in my ears.

Shaking my head, I'm confused.

Did I dream that? The house, the heads, the chicken scratch etched into the walls?

"I don't know. I don't know…" My voice trembles as I continue repeating myself.

"Hey, hey. Dexy, it's ok. I got you, mama has got you." She reassures me, still not letting go. Then her tone changes, she's speaking directly to Jasper now, "If they did this. I will fucking kill them. And it will be even more fun than Sutton." She finishes with a giggle.

Reaching my hand up, I touch mama's, lightly tapping as a signal that I'm ready to get up. The comfort of her hold is gone. Following suit, I rise and see mama's hand reaching out. Grabbing it softly, I wrap my large hand around hers. Jasper takes her other one, and we walk in silence back to the barn.

My mind isn't resting. I don't fucking understand, how did I end up here? My fist closes and begins pounding into the side of my head while a loud scream breaks free from between my lips. Mama lets go of my other hand and places both hands on my face, attempting to bring me back to center me.

"Sweet boy, please talk to me." Her voice pleads.

My words come out stuttering, "I don't know…"

Because I fucking don't.

Leaning into her touch, I stop pounding.

It wasn't real. It wasn't real.

Shut up, shut up, shut up!

Dex Ashford, formally Dex Ryan, who was also formally Dexter John Walters. Born on October 7th to two drug addict parents. Later sold at the age of ten to the Ryan family, who you may know as mom and dad, for drug money. And the sole purpose of the Ryan's acquiring you...

"NO. It wasn't real!"

More flashes of my past are coming to the forefront.

"Dex. Buddy. Can you drink this for me? It will help." Jasper's voice sounds like it is miles away, echoing.

With shaking hands, I reach out, gripping the cool cup. Mama steps out of the way, but I still feel her. With one large inhale, I drink every last drop.

"Crushed sleeping pills into the water." Jasp tells Mama. She doesn't object.

"Let's get you to bed, sweet boy."

Nodding, I follow my family into the barn. My eyes begin to feel droopy as I take slow, heavy steps up the wooden stairs. Each movement takes extra effort, it's hitting me immediately.

The last thing I remember is falling face first onto my bed and falling asleep.

CHAPTER 8
LIAM

"What the fuck is wrong with you?"

Izzie is screaming at the top of her tiny lungs. Rolling my eyes, I light the joint between my lips. Taking a hit, I blow out a large cloud of smoke that only further irritates her.

"Was any of that even true, or did you make it all up?"

Ignoring her, I continue scratching the wall with my latest piece.

> *As the devil dances*
> *Angels sing sweet screams of sorrow*

"LIAM!"

> *As their light fades*
> *The devil smiles*

We always win, never escaping death, sweet angels

"Liam, fucking answer me!" Izzie screeches, as I continue writing.

You are home now

"I meant every fucking word. Everything has a paper trail. In case it took more effort to get you back, I had it waiting. Sitting in my back pocket. But I didn't need it. Until tonight. He welcomed himself into our home, and I didn't want to be a rude host." I casually explain to my little sister. Her green eyes may as well be red, she is furious. She is so fucking sexy like this.

"You fucking prick!"

Chuckling back at her, "You like my giant prick, sweet baby sister."

Taking my pen, I add a few designs next to the words freshly written, a few 'X's and devil horns. Once finished, I take another hit off my joint, and as I blow it out, I look over to Izzie. Her arms are crossed over her chest as she shakes her head at me.

"On your knees. Take my cock out." I instruct, looking her up and down. Her eyes widen in disgust, "You must be out of your fucking mind."

Stepping forward, I reach my hand out and wrap my fingers around her tiny throat, pushing her against the wall. Looking down at her, through gritted teeth, "On your knees."

She swallows, her bright green eyes look back up at me in defiance.

A smirk spreads on her face, "No."

I squeeze her neck harder, and Izzie coughs as I restrict her breathing. With my joint still between my lips, I take one more hit. Once I deeply inhale, I let it fall to the ground, still lit at our feet. My lips touch hers; she hates weed, but I don't fucking care. Her head tries to move, but I don't let her. Pressing my lips hard against hers, I blow the smoke out. It penetrates between her lips and even moves up her nose.

My hand releases from her throat, and her body automatically reacts, searching for fresh air. She takes even more weed in instead.

Izzie's hand slaps against my bare arm, it stings. "Fuck you!"

Fine, I will.

Spinning her around as dry coughs fill the space, her hands brace themselves against the hallway wall where she's been yelling at me this entire time.

"In my defense, I didn't do anything to him. He left here screaming 'mama, mama' all on his own after he snooped." I explain as I kick her legs apart. She is in a sleep shirt, which I have bunched up now, exposing her bare ass.

"Always fucking ready for me," I hiss in her ear.

A shiver travels down her body; she trembles under my words.

Grinding my hard cock against her, her breath hitches as her back arches. It is restricted by my pants, but seeing her response to me further ignites the fire within. Letting her go, I swiftly unzip my pants and pull my cock out. Rubbing my thumb over my head, precum is already dripping.

Izzie sticks her pert ass out, inviting me in; her sleep shirt rides up, exposing her delicious flesh. Wasting no time, I position my cock between her dripping, swollen lips. Circling my head around her entrance only further stimulates her sensitive pussy. Izzie's forehead rests against the wall; she's high and horny. Her body is screaming at her as her nerves tingle in desire.

My sweet sister.

I slam into her, and a moan escapes her.

My lips brush against her hair, which is covering her ear, "I'm not sorry."

Both hands grip around her hips as I take control, using her for my own release. I don't doubt that she will get off, her walls are already gripping me tightly.

Our breathing is heavy as I continue fucking her.

My voice rasps firmly, "Next time I tell you to get on your knees, you fucking do it."

"I will, I promise."

"Next time, I will drug you with more than weed, and I will take what I fucking want that way. Do you understand?"

"Ah, yes. Yes. I understand. Please keep going. Don't stop, Liam," Izzie moans, unable to hold in her yearning, her need.

She knows I'm not fucking around.

I continue fucking her tight cunt, she is soaking as she squeezes my cock tightly inside of her. My movements become more rapid as I feel my orgasm approaching. Izzie's whimpers set me over, ropes of my cum begin to fill her. Her head falls back, and her pussy pulsates as she chases her own. My legs shake and my toes tingle.

This fucking girl is mine.

Heavy breathing fills the hall. I wrap my arm around her, holding my sister closer to me as the final drops of my cum empty into her. Izzie's head falls on my shoulders, her eyes are heavy and glazed. I reach my hand down her front, my thumb and forefinger find her clit, and I squeeze it tightly. Her pelvis bucks and her pussy grips me tighter.

Izzie's fingers rake through my thick white hair, gripping the roots at the base, she pulls it hard. I smile, loving the pain.

"You love me." I confidently tell her.

Izzie bites her bottom lip, still in a daze, "Fucking always."

CHAPTER 9
DEX

Waking up today, I still wasn't sure what was real and what my mind tricked me into seeing and believing.

I'm sitting watching the meadow—the same meadow mama and Jasper found me in. Still confused, I'm staring at the center. How did I get there?

My vision is hyper focused.

Then white fluffy pollen tickles my nose, and a sneeze escapes.

"Dex?"

It's Izzie.

Fuck. When did she get here?

How does she know it's me?

"It's ok, I won't hurt you. Please don't leave."

My eyes look around, but it doesn't take long to notice, she is standing directly next to me.

Wearing a white linen sundress, no shoes and her

matching sunhat, her green eyes look down upon me while her red hair is tied behind her.

As long as she doesn't touch me, I'll be ok.

I repeat this to myself as I wait for her to continue. My demeanor doesn't change, I don't want to startle her. Last time she ran away from me. I can't let her run away again. She means too much.

"My brother...he is protective. Territorial. Um... a dick." A sweet giggle follows. The corner of my mouth lifts, wanting to smirk. But I can't. No. I cannot let her in. Showing her my emotions will show her my weaknesses. It's a risk. I don't want to believe she will hurt me or use them against me, but the past is currently defining me.

"It's ok. You are safe with me."

Liar.

Is my instant reaction. Only mama keeps me safe.

Her face changes, her mouth frowns, and sadness washes over her. "You left so quickly the other night. He was out of line; I'm sorry."

It was real.

No. No. No.

Sliding my hands into my hood, I grip my hair, pulling it tightly until it stings.

Shut up. Shut up. Shut up.

My eyes squeeze shut as I rock against the strong tree trunk.

It's true. Why else would he say it?

What I saw was real.

What I felt was fucking real.

What I heard... *No, no, no.*

Izzie's hand touches my shoulder, it burns through my sweater.

Shaking her off, I crawl on my hands and knees, moving feet away from her.

"I'm sorry. I shouldn't have... I should have known." Izzie has curled into herself. She doesn't seem sad. She seems more taken back, rejected.

"Do you sit here often? Watching me?" She asks in an attempt to change the subject. I don't respond, and my body continues to shake.

Her eyes look down, uncomfortable by my silence.

I want to get up and run. I don't want to be alone with her anymore.

"He's going away for a couple days. My brother, Liam. He should be gone now, actually. Do you maybe want to try it again?"

My brows furrow in confusion.

"Hanging out. Isn't that why you were at the house last night?" She asks curiously.

Don't let your past define you.

Don't let your past define you.

But it fucking does.

Shaking my head, I refuse; I don't want to go anywhere near that house again. It doesn't stop her. Izzie takes a step forward, and I take an inch back.

"I won't hurt you. I promise."

She repeats the same line from earlier.

Liar.

"Please." Her voice is weak, calculated, and manipulative.

"I'm not playing you." She responds as if she is reading my thoughts.

My brain is running rampant with conflicting thoughts. I'm not a coward. But I also don't know if I can trust her. Why does she want to take me home? What if her brother is waiting for me, and she is the bait to get me to him?

Before I can sort and analyze her motive, her angle, my body reacts to her invitation.

With a racing heart, my legs respond on their own accord, rising. With my hands in my pockets, my head nods once. My eyes stay at my feet; I am unable to see her reaction, but I can hear her feet move against the earth and I follow.

Against all my better judgement, I fucking follow.

Worst case, she is lying. It is a trap; I kill them both. Him first, make her watch, make her feel pain and hopefully it would make her cry.

I would then spend days torturing her. Grinning, it takes me back to Sutton. That infamous night that led us here.

I would burn the bitch down over and over again.

Hurting makes me happy. It's therapeutic. And thinking of it now lifts my spirits immensely.

By the time I look up, we are standing at her back door as she opens it for us. Following, I step inside. The kitchen is bright in the daylight. White cabinets with dark countertops and flooring decorate the area. The etched words adorn the walls, which I remember vividly from last night. Then my eyes find the fridge, and my arm raises as my finger points to it.

Izzie's response is casual, "That's my brother's thing." Looking at her, she shrugs her shoulders like it's no big deal. Similar to how mama would, when people would whisper about her and Jasper fucking in front of Mr. H. Skipping along, she would shrug her shoulders without a single fuck to give and say, *'We are the Queen and King of Sutton. We make the rules. And what Mr. H wants, he gets.'*

"What is that mute fuck doing here?"

My immediate reaction is, mama. My heart beat picks up, shocked and panic-stricken.

I fucking knew it. She played me.

"Yeah, go tell your mama what a bad fucking boy I have been." He taunts.

It's Liam.

"Liam. Stop! Why are you here? You said you were leaving." Izzie's tone is defensive and protective.

He laughs at her, leaning against the opening with his legs crossed and wearing a black crop top with black jeans and sneakers. Ink covers his exposed skin, and his thick white hair hangs over his forehead. His lips are full and smirking while his dark eyes look into mine.

"I am leaving. Izzie, mute, I bid you farewell." His

voice changed from lazy to formal as he turns on his heel and walks away.

"Let's go to my room."

My head shakes at her suggestion.

"Living room?"

I nod my head once and follow her.

Walking through the archway Liam just left leads us to an open space, dark furniture, a television, and more white walls with black words scratched all over them.

Izzie whispers, noticing me taking in the walls, "Also my brother's thing."

If Sutton allowed patients to have markers, no doubt the walls would have looked like this as well. White walls full of chaotic lettering and art decorate the house.

I wonder if the entire place is like this.

We sit; she's on a large, oversized chair next to the couch I take residence on.

"He shouldn't have told you that way. He shouldn't have told you at all." Her eyes look sad as she says the last word. Perhaps the empathy is real.

So it is true.

My chest tightens, and my mind races. I was born to be sold, to be used. I was sold to people who knew exactly what would happen to me, and they let it. Never feeling bad, never intervening. Anger and rage flow through my veins the longer I contemplate it. They shouldn't have been shocked to find *her* skinned alive and dead on the floor. What do you expect when you push a person night after night?

Tick Tock on the clock brings memories flooding back.

Sitting on her as I peel her skin back inch by inch. It should have been them, too.

I wonder how much they paid. Maybe they just threw drugs at my birth parents to close the deal. With a tight fist, I punch the cushion, only once. I only allow myself to feel pity for that one punch.

My past does not define me.

What's done is done.

My past does not define me.

"If this is too much, you can go." Izzie suggests. My eyes look at her inquisitively.

"My brother, he acts tough, but I know he sees what I do, he doesn't know how to feel. So he feels the only way he knows how. By acting like a dick. But you're gentle. You are kind. You are cherished. And you are so fucking strong."

Don't mistake my kindness for weakness. These compliments have me wondering if she does.

"You have been through so much. You three are infamous for what happened at Sutton. It's half the reason the town hasn't said anything, I think. The other half is, they hope if they leave you all alone, you will return the favor." She pauses, giggling into her hand, "The town hopes that of my brother too."

She's opening up.

"They see me as the sweet one, him as the scary one. It doesn't bother us." Izzie pauses, biting her lip before continuing, "Did you tell them...about what Liam said?"

I shake my head, as my eyes move towards the kitchen, not allowing her to change the subject. I know what I saw. Severed heads draining in the fridge. I want to know more.

"Liam kills them, then eats them."

The fuck? I don't move; her response wasn't one I ever expected. My mind wanders; so many questions and thoughts race through me. The only one I can focus on is, I wonder if they know Ms. O.

CHAPTER 10
IZZIE

Dex didn't stay long after I dropped the bomb about Liam. He didn't show any emotion after what I had exposed, I trust him though. Something about him is telling me it's okay. He is safe. And not because he is mute. Dex has been exposed to the most vile things and been around people more depraved than my brother's hobbies. Knowing just a taste of what Liam does didn't phase him once.

Before he left, raindrops tapped on the windows, and Dex became more agitated as we sat together in silence. His eyes focused more on the clock. Eventually, his leg was bouncing so rapidly that he stood up and briskly left. The closing of the screen door behind him indicated that he was gone.

That was a couple days ago. I'm arranging the fresh flowers from the meadow on the kitchen table as I hear my brother's car roaring up the driveway. Dex was there. I felt him watching me, but I let him be, to not push him further.

I'll be the first to admit, my brother was an absolute asshole for telling Dex all that shit about his past. Just throwing it out without any warning; it was one of the coldest things I had ever witnessed him do. They are more similar than they think. Liam doesn't have a filter and just spits shit out before thinking, empathy isn't a distinct trait within him. Dex is methodical; what he lacks in words, he shows in his behavior. And both feel really fucking deeply. How they express it is different.

My brother scratches poetry on the walls, protects me, and loves me even if he doesn't communicate it. Dex observes, nurtures, loves, and feels down deep into his core. He is more fragile and timid, but like Liam, he isn't afraid to fuck shit up. It's interesting watching them both. Even if it's only a couple times. Body language can say more than words.

"Get the mute," Liam shouts with his head poking through the backdoor.

Tucking my long red hair behind my ear, I turn to face him, confused, "What?" His signature *'up to no good'* grin is making an appearance. What the fuck has he done?

I'm apprehensive, he can tell.

"I'm not going to hurt him, baby sister. You're intrigued by him for whatever fucking reason." Liam rolls his eyes sarcastically. Is he jealous?

"Big brother, are you displeased by this?" I question with curiosity. Liam throws his head back in a fit of laughter, "Absolutely not. You're never fucking leaving me for a mute. He's not a threat. But, I do have a peace offering for you, sweet sister, and your new bestie. Now stop fucking around and go get him. I promise, it's not a trap."

With his last word, he leaves. The backdoor closes and I don't know what to think. A peace offering? Shaking my head slightly, I reach for my sun hat, which is resting on the table, and place it on top of my head. My feet pad out of the kitchen and out the backdoor.

Shouting back as I scurry away, "I'll kill you if you're lying to me, Liam!"

DEX

Three loud knocks echo throughout the wooden barn. Mama is lying on my bed with me; her fingers are tangled in my hair as I rest my eyes. She's worried about me. I haven't said anything about Izzie since the night she found me in the meadow with Jasp. To be fair, I'm not sure what to say about it. It was only confirmed to me that what I saw was real, and I'm not sure what I am to do with this information.

Two more knocks riddle the place. We still don't move.

The loud sound of the barn door sliding open fills

the space. I know both mama and I are listening closely; we don't get visitors.

"Um, is Dex home?" The familiar voice is faintly tickling my ears. A loud huff comes from mama; her fingers stop moving, and her legs are over the edge by the time I look over to her.

Stomping out of my room, she leans over the balcony, "Oh, the skank is back!" She shouts gleefully.

Fuck.

This is not good.

Scurried feet pad down the wooden stairs. Throwing my own legs over the side of my bed, I follow. Making my way down, I look up and see Izzie wide-eyed as mama hurries over to her. It all happens so quickly. Mama's hand reaches out, tossing Izzie's sunhat off, then grips her long red hair, sunkissed with strawberry blonde streaks, and begins pounding her freckled face against the wooden barn door in quick succession, one after another.

High-pitched screams of terror follow. I freeze. Jasp reacts as mama taunts my pretty girl, "Stupid fucking skank. I found him in the meadow, destroyed. What did you do?!"

Jasp wraps his arms around mama and pulls her back, "Savage, I think she gets it. Let's take it easy."

Scratching my arm out of discomfort, I freeze as I realize I don't have my sweater on. I'm not safe around her. I barely notice the blood dripping out of Izzie's nose and down her face. Panic sets in, my chest heaves with anxiety, *please make her leave.*

Izzie's voice tries to penetrate my racing thoughts, "My brother and I were wondering if Dex could come over for a bit? Hang out."

My head shakes no, not stopping.

"Fuck his sweater. Savage, I need to help him. Don't hurt her, please."

I feel someone running past me as my vision blurs.

Next thing I feel is the warm embrace of my sweater being pulled over my head and down my body. My arms slide in the sleeves, which automatically begins to calm me. My breathing evens out, and the scene before me becomes clear.

Izzie is bleeding down her chin, and it is dripping onto her pale sundress. Mama has her arms crossed over her chest with her head tilted, looking at her.

"It's okay, buddy. She had to do it."

I know she did. That family hurt me; so mama did what she does best.

Defending ours.

"Did you want to hang out with her? It's okay if you do. If shit goes south, you know the plan. You know what to do and where to meet us. We always got you," Jasp whispers so only I can hear.

Doing a quick nod, I flip my hood over my head and walk toward the barn door.

Mama growls at Izzie as I reach her.

Pulling mama into a warm embrace, I reassure her with one squeeze. Her body relaxes into our hug as she rubs her hand on my back.

As I step back, we make eye contact, and she's telling me the same thing Jasp did. Then with a nostril flare, she adds the hint that I should just take Izzie and her brother out, too, if needed. Walking away, I turn my head back and wink and head outside.

Passing Izzie, she seems surprised I have come so willingly; so am I frankly, but what is life without risk? Plus, I want to know more. I need to know more.

CHAPTER 11
LIAM

Leaning against the cool cement wall, with a joint lit between my lips, waiting for our guest of honor. Izzie is my good little slut, and she stays good as long as I keep her happy. She seems to have grown some sort of fondness towards the mute; therefore, I went to find the perfect peace offering, which hopefully will result in her slobbering on my cock later.

Hearing the back door close tells me she is back, but did he come?

My question is answered when I hear two sets of feet making their way to the basement. The area is dark, windows blacked out with only a single lightbulb on, which is swinging over my new friends.

Izzie's delicate face peeks out of the stairwell, "Liam. It's safe, right?"

Smart sister. Protecting the mute.

Rolling my eyes, I lazily respond to her stupid fucking question, "I told you it would be."

"Say it!"

Feisty.

"It's safe. I'm not going to hurt your bestie." I sigh while blowing out a cloud of smoke.

My sister reveals herself, walking into the open space, with the mute behind her staring down at his feet as he follows.

I catch the moment her eyes see what is before her. They widen, knowing what will happen next. Then confusion follows, "Who are they?"

A loud, cruel laugh emerges from my mouth as I take a step forward. Throwing my arms open with my head thrown back, I shout, "Dexter, tell the good people. Who are these fine folks before us?"

"The dramatics. Are they really fucking necessary, Liam?" Oh, my sister has no patience.

Bringing my head back up, I lower my arms, throwing my joint to the ground and stomping it out. My eyes bypass Izzie and zone in immediately on Dex, who isn't phased by my question; his eyes remain focused at his feet.

That just won't do.

Taking a few steps forward, I bypass my sister, whose nose is a bloody fucking mess, "Sister, you should clean that up."

A displeased growl leaves her, "No shit."

Dare I say this new attitude is also her being protective?

Rubbing my chest over my black mesh crop, I can feel my nipples harden at her tone. She is definitely sucking my dick later.

The tip of my shoes meets *his.* As they do, he tries to move back, but I reach out, stopping him. His body tenses under my touch, "Tell us, who are they?"

"Liam, please. He isn't like us. Be gentle." Izzie pleads.

Bull-fucking-shit.

I've read what he did to his sister. Then at Sutton. He is exactly like us.

I don't say it out loud; it will only start an argument. Instead, I keep my focus on him.

"Look at me." I demand through gritted teeth.

His chin is vibrating as his head slowly moves up. As it does, his eyes meet mine. Dark, lonely, dangerous.

I encourage him once more, "Who?"

Long lashes touch his cheek briefly with each blink. His focus moves to behind me, which causes him to startle. Jolting back, a gasp escapes him. Shock is decorating his face.

Good boy. Now tell us, who are they?

"You're upsetting him. You promised Liam!"

"Izzie, shut the fuck up for two seconds."

She's going to ruin it! This is important.

"Shut up, shut up, shut up." Is all the mute says while taking his balled fist to the side of his head.

Izzie rushes over, reaching for his hand and he screams, "No!"

"Wow, sister. I got this. Step back." I instruct. Knowing his history, I'm not a complete neanderthal. He is not going to want her to touch him.

"Mute, she isn't going to touch you. But you need to face your fucking fears, bro."

"Shut up, shut up, shut up."

Reaching out, I grip his face with both my ink-covered hands and pull his focus back onto me. "Look at me. Stop, breathe, and just look at me," I whisper through heavy breaths. My own heart is racing at the intensity of this moment.

With a quivering lip, he gives me a curt nod.

"Good boy. Now look at me and tell me who they are."

I don't let go, keeping him centered and focused on only me.

"They are asleep. They don't even know you are here."

Taking a deep breath in, I expect him to finally speak up, but he doesn't. Instead, he looks around the space. Placing his hands on my arms, he lowers them off his face, gently, then scurries over to the cement wall I was just leaning against.

Using his finger, he begins to draw.

It's shaky and hard to figure out at first.

Between each letter, he whispers, "Shut up."

T
H
E

My eyes carefully follow each movement.
He is telling us.
Adrenaline is buzzing through me.

R
Y
A
N
'
S

Izzie's hands cover her mouth in shock. At the same time, I praise our mute, "Good boy."

"Do you want to play with them, with me?"

His head whips in my direction with hooded eyes.

With a single nod, it's time.

DEX

Laid out on two wooden folding tables are my mom and dad. The Duct Tape is tightly secured around their naked bodies, including the tops of their heads. Both are asleep and unaware.

"Anything you want, do it." The words are whispered into the cold space.

I don't understand. Why are they here?

If what Liam said is true, they aren't my parents. My parents were addicts. It could help explain my compulsive need to watch Izzie. A day without and not scheduled makes my skin itch. If it is true that these two people lying here bought me, used me then left me to hang, then it's only fair I return the favor. Exactly like what I did to *her* and Karen.

More thoughts are running rampant in my mind. Squeezing my eyes shut, I need it to stop. The tick of a clock causes my body to react. My neck snaps to where it is coming from as I open my eyes, fully alert.

Liam.

Liam is holding a metal pocket watch in his hands. A giant smirk adorns his face; he knows.

Shut up, shut up, shut up.

I can still feel the rope between my fingers.

Stretching my fingers out, I try to shake the feeling.

Taking a step forward, I cover my ears. I need it to stop.

They have aged. Their skin is more droopy, and wrinkles cover their faces. As my eyes scan down their bodies, I notice the parts wrapped are beginning to turn purple and blue from lack of circulation. How long have they been like this?

I'm startled as Liam comes to stand next to me; his shoulder touches mine and I growl, letting him know I don't like it. He places his hands in front of me, showing me the pocket watch is gone. I shake my head, and he points towards where he was once standing. Following his finger, I see it; he has smashed it. The *tick tock* is gone; it's safe.

"A peace offering."

My face scrunches in confusion as I look at him. Liam's eyes penetrate mine, it nearly takes my breath away. It feels uncomfortable, but I don't move. My chest fills with warmth the longer we stay like this; it's unsettling.

"Anything you want." He repeats his earlier statement.

Using the table, my eyes move to where I placed my finger on top of it. His focus follows mine; I can feel it.

With still shaking fingers, I write, 'Is it true? Did they buy me?'

After the last question mark, I look back up at him and wait. Liam's breathing is heavy, I can see his chest moving beneath his mesh crop top. His face changes from one of excitement and revenge to sorrow and sympathy. He moves his eyes back to my finger and gives one curt nod. A sigh of relief exhales out of my lungs. The truth is better than lies, even if the truth is fucking horrific.

Sharp teeth bite the inside of my lip. The taste of copper dances along the taste buds of my tongue. The warm blood in my veins is pleading with me to allow this release. Flipping my hand over, I expose my palm.

A single silver razor blade is gently placed into it.

Closing my hand tightly around it, I feel it pierce my skin with a sting. Taking another deep breath in, I position myself over my mom's head. If it was anyone's idea, it was hers. Then once selling my dad on the idea, that's when it would have happened.

"Don't think about it. Just do it," Liam coaxes.

Taking the bloodied blade between my fingers, I angle it down over the thin skin of her closed eyes. Pushing down, the sharp metal slices the skin beautifully. Crimson red beads just before dripping down the side of her face. Dragging the blade across the lid, I continue the cut. The room is silent as I focus on the parting skin. The further I go, you begin to see more of the whites from her eyeball. Reaching the corner of the lid, I use my other hand to grip the lashes between my fingers and lift the disconnected piece of skin off of her face.

Fascinated, I examine what I just did. Her eyes are rolled into the back of her head. Why didn't she wake?

"I didn't give them a lot, they will both wake up soon and once they do, it won't be as quiet." Liam's words answer my question, they were drugged.

Gingerly, I place the thin piece of eyelid flat on the table and move to the next. Starting from the corner, I place the tip of the blade into the skin and begin sliding it through. It's like butter, an effortless cut as I reach the end. Doing the same with this lid, I place it down flat on the table and rest the blade next to them.

Fuck, it feels good. My mouth is salivating with desire to continue.

"I think we should wake her up now." Liam chuckles.

Watching him intently, he shows me exactly what he means.

The tips of his chipped, polished fingers dig into her eye socket, gripping her eyeball tightly. With a single flick of the wrist, he is able to dislodge it. *Has he done this before?*

Still attached to the ball are the muscles, arteries and nerves.

"Be a good boy and cut me free?"

Taking the razor back in my hand, I cut anything I can see that is connecting the eye to the socket, including the primary vein providing the blood supply. It squirts and splatters once sliced. The socket, which is initially a beautiful piece of muscles and tissue, is quickly filling with blood. Looking up at Liam, he winks at me before popping the eyeball into his mouth.

I wince as I see his sharp white teeth bite down into it. A mixture of saliva and blood glistens down his chin as he continues to chew into it.

Moving it side to side, I can see it protruding out of his cheeks—a perfect circular ball. It reminds me of one of those giant gumballs from those machines when I was a kid, a jawbreaker.

He eventually gets into a rhythm. I'm not sure how long it takes, but the large round ball becomes chunks in his mouth. Liam's throat moves with each swallow. Sticking out his tongue, his teeth are stained red to match the dribble still moving down his chin onto his shirt. It's gone. He ate it.

Snapping his fingers, he smirks, "Izzie. Clean me up."

Sweet Izzie scurries over, eager to please her brother. Gripping his face, she sticks her tongue out and licks his jawline, then lets go and bends over. Starting at his exposed belly button, her tongue dances in it. Lapping any excess juices before slowly moving up his tattooed stomach, then up his mesh top. Moans of delight leave her. She likes this.

Liam's nipples are still erect as I take in the sight before me.

Fuck.

I look up at him; he catches me. Our eyes meet just like before. My chest tightens with need.

What is happening to me?

Fisting Izzie's long hair, he pulls it down, causing her face to look up. His lips crash into hers, and he devours her while keeping eye contact with me.

My cock tingles. Pulsating against my shorts.

His arm moves, pulling her off him, "Stand on top of her." Izzie giggles in response, then jumps on top of the table, standing spread legged over my mom's head. Her body is facing me as she waits for her next instruction, but it doesn't come.

Liam walks over, and I step aside, giving him access to her.

Placing two fingers in his mouth, he coats them with his saliva, then slips them underneath her short, flowing sundress. A faint, "Fuck," slips off the tip of her tongue as her eyes hood.

He finger bangs her relentlessly; the faster he goes, the more her legs quiver.

"Slap her face. Wake her up."

Removing my focus from them, I look down at my mom. I don't want to touch her. I can't touch her with my hands. My body tenses before noticing the blade is still sitting, waiting for me to use it again.

Taking it, I place it under her nose and slice the septum, hoping it feels exactly like a paper cut stinging across her skin.

It doesn't work.

Peering down at her lips, I take the tip and trace along her lip line, making the cut as deep as I can possibly make it.

Relief lifts off my body. I desperately needed this and didn't even know it.

But *he* did.

Slicing the corners before moving to her bottom lip, a loud gasp exits her. Mom's awake. Stepping back with the blade still in hand, I'm taken aback, shocked and surprised. It was easier when she was unconscious.

"Izzie, squat for me, my sweet filthy whore." Liam's voice rasps.

Screams of pain send shivers down my spine.

They sound like *hers*.

"Fuck, Liam. It's too much. The pressure. I can't take it." She whimpers as her knees touch the table, trembling with desire.

A loud slap follows, "You will fucking take it. Hike up your dress, let Dex see." He pauses while she adjusts her dress, "Dex, you want to watch, don't you?"

More moans follow as his fingers work her pussy. The palm of his hand rubs against her clit. She grips her hair lightly; she is unsure what to do with them as the ecstasy builds inside.

"Ah, Liam."

Then it gushes out like nothing I have ever seen before as it fills the empty eye socket. Is she pissing? It's hard to tell in the dim lighting.

"Yes, keep going. Fuck."

"Does my filthy whore like when I do this? Making you squirt all over this sack of shit?"

"God, yes. It feels so fucking good."

Once it stops coming out of her, she is panting loudly. Her eyes are closed as she catches her breath. Hands are shaking as Liam removes himself from under her dress and moves them under her arms to help her down.

Izzie is limp.

Placing her on the ground, she lays on her side.

"It always makes her tired after." Liam explains.

Mom is still screaming.

He looks up at me, "You do it or I will."

I nod once more, blade still in hand, as I walk back towards the table.

"Dex, our sweet Dex." She sounds like a blubbering idiot. I believe Liam. He has no reason to lie to me. When he told me he wanted to hurt me. It was the truth.

Pushing the razor through the skin of her throat, I push hard. Blood immediately coats my fingers the harder I go, but I don't let up. Pushing and sliding it slowly across her flesh. Blood trickles down, pooling around either side of her.

She coughs up a clot of blood; I've hit the artery.

Not much time left now. Her body is already numb from the lack of circulation.

Reaching the other side of her throat, I let go of the blade, leaving it dug deep inside of her. Bending over, my lips hover over her ear as I whisper, "*She* screamed so beautifully."

CHAPTER 12
LIAM

My mute likes to play with my food. And I like watching him.

These motherfuckers aren't getting off this easy.

Daddy dearest eyes flutter as he comes out of his drug coma.

"And in case you're wondering what happened to your brother, I chopped him up and loaded him into my freezer." I clap my hands as I spin on my heels towards Dex.

He is a fiend; I can smell his need for more. His dad is mumbling nonsense behind me, a mixture of the drugs and hearing what I did to his kid, surely.

"We will leave him to suffer next to his rotting, dead whore of a wife."

Dex stands silently. His hands resting on either side

of him, coated in crimson as it drips off him onto the floor.

Red is really his color.

Spinning back around, I hop effortlessly onto the wooden table supporting his dad. Tilting my head, I look down upon him, tears run down his cheeks as he incoherently rambles in grief.

"You, my friend, are my peace offering. My sister has taken a liking to the mute, therefore I have. Your family is dead. You are alive. You should feel horrible inside. But I don't. He-" I pause and point to Dex, "Doesn't. But you should."

Lowering my hand, I move it to unlatch my pants' button and unzip my zipper. I'm not wearing underwear, so my cock is an easy reach. Gripping it casually in my hand, I aim it over this fucker's face and release the waterfalls, pissing all over his face.

"Drink up. It's all you will be getting for a while."

He is unable to move, like his whore of a wife. I secured the tape tightly down at the forehead. My piss falls over his lips, into his eyes, and all over his nose and hair. Some makes it into his mouth as he moans in disgust. It's very rude. The stream thins, I shake my cock and the last couple drops dribble out. Tucking myself back in, I do my pants back up and hop down. Slapping the table with my hand, Dex jumps.

Shit.

Holding up both hands, I show him I mean no harm. His shoulders relax and his brows lower.

Bending down, I finger the loose hair on Izzie's face away, "Izzie, wake up. Time to take Dex home. This was enough for one day. And I'm starving." Having the mute watch me down the eyeball was a risk. He doesn't need to watch me feast on their flesh.

My sister rolls over, then props herself up, her hair is disheveled and her eyes are barely open. Standing, she gives her body a shake, something she does to help wake herself up. Adjusting her dress as she rises, Izzie pads towards the stairwell, the mute follows without a single word or goodbye. Within moments, they disappear up the stairs and the backdoor can be heard closing behind them.

Reaching over daddy Ryan, I coat my hand in his dead wife's blood. Pulling my reach back, I let some blood drop onto his face, "She screamed like a bitch."

Loud sobs echo. I take the opportunity to flick some blood into his mouth, only further escalating his sweet screams of sorrow.

Lifting my hand up to my face, I place my palm on my cheek and slowly slide it down my jaw and over my collarbone. It's warm, thick, and smells of rusted metal. My skin ignites. It loves being coated in it. Sticking my fingers into my mouth, sweet iron dances on my tongue.

"Fuck," I hiss.

Turning away, I make my way out of the basement, leaving the single light on, so daddy Ryan can always keep his dead wife in his peripheral view.

The smell of savory stew takes over my senses. I put it in the crockpot before Izzie and the mute arrived.

Opening the glass lid, the smell becomes stronger. A mixture of garden fresh potatoes, carrots, and peas mixed in with a blood gravy and cubed chucks of the mutes brothers' thick and juicy thigh. I don't wait, taking the large mixing spoon, I scoop a large portion onto it. Steam floats off, too impatient to wait, I take a deep breath and blow on it. The steam drifts away, and I shove it in my mouth.

So fucking good.

The meat is cooked to perfection, tender and chewy. The vegetables complement it well, and the thick blood gravy pulls it all together.

Standing in silence as I eat, my mind wanders down memory lane.

The mute wasn't the only one fucked up by family.

IZZIE

He has blood all over his hands.

If anyone sees us, we are fucked. This is not what we do. We are not this messy, this fucking showy. What has my brother done?

Thoughts run wild in my head, trying to figure out his angle. None of this is making sense.

Neither of us has said a word since leaving the house. We enter the treeline, leaving my meadow behind.

That's when it hits me. A hot wave of realization washes over my body.

My heart drops into the pit of my stomach. *"Shit."* I stop moving, frozen in place.

Dex makes it a couple feet ahead of me before noticing I am no longer behind him. His head turns to face me, he looks confused.

"He sees himself in you," I whisper, while making eye contact with Dex. His expression has remained unchanged.

Blowing out a deep sigh, I continue, "Our dad... he used to hurt Liam. I mean, *really* hurt him. With more than just words. Sometimes there would be so much fucking blood after. It's like he saw my brother as prey in the wild. He would carve him up until he was on the brink, then stop and bring him back to life. He was a surgeon. A fucking mad scientist. Liam sees himself in you. He has never done this before, Dex. Never."

The verbal diarrhea is unstoppable.

"Until one day, when Liam turned the tables." Tears pool in my eyes. I don't know why; the memory doesn't haunt me. Perhaps it's because it's the first time I am saying this shit out loud.

"Our mom, we don't know her. Never have, it's always just been us." The crunching of leaves under Dex's shoes stops me. He is moving closer to me; confusion has turned to concern and interest.

"Hours, maybe days, I don't remember. Liam slowly killed him. Stabbing my dad with adrenaline anytime he was on the brink of passing out or dying. Liam used knives, scalpels, and carving forks. Stabbing and cutting just deep enough to draw a steady stream of red, like your hands." I pause, taking a deep breath before continuing, "Then gluing the lacerations closed, just to pick them off later. His entire body was covered. Liam wanted him to feel what he felt. He had my dad tied down just like the Ryan's. He is going to make your dad hurt, *really*, really hurt, Dex."

Dex stomps at me, his face in mine, rage is radiating off him. His eyes appear black as his chest heaves, shaking his head insistently. But I am not scared.

"I'm sorry. Not your dad. You're right. Iris and Jasper are your family." I say apologetically, not standing down to him.

His body relaxes, then his face follows.

"Once he finally ended my dad, he didn't stop there. Liam continued, butchering him up like a deer after a kill. This was his first. The heads in the fridge you saw, his most recent until today. Liam is tortured. So fucking beautifully tortured. Just like you, Dex. He expresses his emotions, loudly. Where you whisper them silently."

Shaking my head in disbelief, it all makes so much sense now.

We stay like this for a few moments. Both absorbing my words. Words I have never said out loud. It's freeing. I feel lighter. A burden no longer only shared with me.

The significance isn't lost on me. None of this happened by chance or luck.

We all, including the twins, are connected.

The moment is broken when Dex turns on his heels and continues walking through the trees. Bringing myself back, I shake my head and follow. The silence is back.

As we reach the end of the thick forest, a cool breeze washes over us. Dex steps out first; I am right behind him as the barn comes into view. The door is already open, and Iris is no doubt nearby, able to smell her cub returning back to the cave. The breeze most definitely carried my scent to her.

I am her prey.

Immediately I go into high alert. The bitch got me once; I won't let her again. Rubbing my hand over my face, the dry blood is still stuck on my skin from our last encounter. Where is she?

"You skanky ass bitch! Why does he have blood on him? What did you make him do?"

My eyes try to find her, following the direction where her voice came from, but I see nothing. I feel it before I hear it. Hands tug on my hair, hurling me to the hard ground. My head bounces twice, and a headache immediately takes up residence. Iris Ashford's foot is now stepping on my stomach, with her crazy eyes glaring viciously down on me.

As I go to speak, Dex places one of his blood-coated hands on her forearm, and his lips whisper, "Mama." A tiny shake of his head is all she needs. Reluctantly, she removes her heavy foot off my abdomen.

I want to scream, hurt her right back. Meet her level

of crazy. But looking at Dex, his face is soft, and I can't be the one to change that. Not after the evening he has already had to endure unexpectedly.

Standing up, I brush my dress off, which is now covered in dry earth and leaves, and look at Dex, "Can I tell her?"

His face pains, and his body language changes as his shoulders shrug. He nods once. That's all I need.

"His mom, the Ryan's, is no longer with us. His dad isn't far behind. The brother didn't stand a chance. It's the only way my brother knows."

Iris shakes her head, confused; her eyes are daggers looking at me, "Skank. More words. Now."

Looking back at Dex, I wait for permission once more, which he gives me in another nod.

"Dex wasn't always Dex Ryan. He was once Dexter John Walters. Liam, my brother, he did research on you guys once we found out you set up camp here. Dex's birth parents were addicts. The Ryan's knew about their daughter's tendencies and didn't want their biological son harmed, so they acquired Dex from the junkies… to serve one purpose." I stop, unable to continue. The thought makes me want to vomit.

The reaction I get next is not one I anticipated. Iris's face shows sadness, I'm shocked. Is she going to cry?

Her lip pouts as she turns to Dex, "Baby, sweet Dex. And you didn't invite me to help? Mama would have loved a piece of that fuck you pie. I'm getting horny just thinking about what fun we could have had destroying her." Her arms cross as her foot stomps.

"Wow, savage. Let's not do that here," Jasper shouts as he comes running out of the barn; I assume he was eavesdropping this entire time. He is never far from her.

"I'll kill the Walters. I have to find them and destroy them. They are why this happened. They are!" As the words fall out of her mouth, she steps into him, wrapping her tiny arms around Dex, who nestles into the crook of her neck.

Iris's mood changes with the wind; it's what makes her so fucking dangerous. From ravenous for revenge to horny to infamous serial killer.

Jasper is standing behind them as he mutters to Iris, "I'll find you someone to hurt, savage. Then I'll fuck you in their blood after."

A muffled purr comes from her briefly before returning her attention back to her Dex.

I stand here watching their interaction. They aren't much different from Liam and I. As I go to leave, Dex raises his head momentarily to wink at me.

My lip curves into a half smile as my eyes continue looking into his, "Come back tomorrow. Whenever you want." I say hopefully, as I leave to go back home. Back to Liam.

Liam who is going to make me pay, I hope, for sharing his secrets.

CHAPTER 13
DEX

What am I doing here?

Why am I so eager to see them again?

The first cut, the blood beading before it trickled down. Euphoric.

Mama was worried, nervous that there could be more at play than we weren't seeing. We did steal his sister, after all. What mama doesn't know is Liam got his revenge; I hear it on repeat in my head every night.

Sold to fuel *their* drug addiction. Sold to feed the hunger of a vermin family member with perverse tastes. Nothing is left. No more cards. Everything is laid out on the table, and I am drawn to it, like a bug to a flame.

Jasp said he was going to do his own research to confirm what the *'skank'* said. My bones feel it's true. The past I have lived is etched inside of me. Any ache or pain, from headaches to bruises, and brief flashes replaying in my mind. It's always in me.

Never quick to trust.

I was apprehensive at first. They made me nervous. They made me curious.

They leave me wanting more. After last night, I need more.

The door opens before I am able to knock; it's Izzie. Her eyes are smiling before it reaches her mouth, she likes me.

"I saw you on the cameras." She is excited to see me.

All I want to do is let her in, from the first day I watched her in the meadow to when she was sitting, helpless, in our cold cellar. Anytime she has tried to penetrate my wall, it's been painful, like hundreds of knives slicing my skin at the same time. I know she only wants to help and bring me comfort, but try telling that to my head.

It's a habit now; my fist is balled as it hits the side of my hard skull. I hate myself sometimes; I hate feeling how I feel or seeing what I see in my mind. It's the only way to make it all stop.

"Dex. Please. Stop..." Her voice sounds pained. She is helpless. "Let's go see Liam. Dex, would you like that? To see my brother?"

The thoughts change at the sound of his name. Images of my mom bleeding out before me begin to flood in. My fist loosens and drops to my side.

Izzie's eyes have changed, worried along with the rest of her face. She doesn't need to. I wish she knew that.

Taking a step forward, she takes one back, turning

around, and she leads me through the kitchen. The back door closes behind us as I follow her up the stairs to the second level. My eyes take in everything. The white walls are covered with more black scratches, exactly like the ones I saw the last time. All the letters are in capitals and look to have been etched out of anger. Anger that needed a release.

We may be surrounded
But I am forever alone

Liam.

"The only places safe from his art are the bathrooms and my room." Izzie confirms his art is his words. Some have pictures around them, others don't. Reaching my fingers out, they glide across the wall, feeling the divots of the carved letters, feeling each letter and the emotion behind it. My throat burns with how deeply it is piercing me.

He hurts too.

Loud music starts to be heard the further we make it up. Walking down the hallway, we don't stop until we reach the closed door at the end of the hall. Izzie doesn't hesitate, turning the knob and pushing it open. Liam is standing by his open window, the sun shining in with a lit joint between his long fingers. Wearing a white tank crop, this time with his signature tight black jeans. His hair looks wet, messy, and hanging over his face.

Blowing out his last puff, Liam's focus remains out the window and mine remains on him.

"She told me about last night. Tsk, tsk, little sister. Revealing your big brother's secrets." His voice is deep, serious, and taunting. Walking over to his desk, he turns the music off and lets the joint sit in his overflowing ashtray.

"He was a piece of shit. Izzie, our sweet girl, always knew how to play him. She learnt early on what would happen if you didn't appease the ol' holy daddy. It's why she's a fucking master at manipulation. She could pout right now and make you feel bad for killing your favorite pet." He chuckles before continuing, "I am what I am. And he is dead because of it. He didn't earn the right to have anything left of him once I was done. After I chopped him up into thirteen perfect pieces, I cooked him in that very kitchen you walked through, then ate him, or what I could. The rest I froze, the bones I dissolved in acid. Like I said, he is a piece of shit."

Liam's lip curls his sharp pearly whites on display.

"Now, back to that naughty girl beside you. On my bed, naked, ass up. Now." He keeps eye contact with me as he speaks to her. My heart is racing. Please don't make me do anything.

"Do you want to watch me eat her pussy?"

I don't respond.

"Or would you rather it be me sucking your cock while she is left dripping with need?"

My breath hitches, not expecting that question.

We both felt it last night; I know we did. But never did I think he would want to act on it? What if I can't?

Liam walks to me slowly; mischief fills the space as Izzie jumps onto his bed. As he reaches me, his musky scent sends a shiver down my spine. Taking a deep breath in, he gets close enough to where I can feel his chest against mine. Leaning into me, his lips move next to my ear. His warm breath dancing on my skin as he whispers, "Not yet, my mute. She would like that punishment too much. Take a seat. Watch. Touch yourself. Get off on it. Be fucking free."

I swallow as my body wants to react. Tingling sensations tickle my skin.

I like it.

As he steps back, his fingers brush against mine. Goosebumps follow as butterflies flutter in my stomach. That's when I move to the lone chair sitting in the corner of his room. It is angled to face the bed, which makes me wonder if it was moved here knowing this could happen. Was this calculated and planned? Was mama right?

No.

Fuck. My balled fist hits my head in quick succession in order to free myself from the paranoid thoughts. I can't help but overthink it.

I catch Liam watching. He doesn't do anything to stop it. Letting my cycle finish. When I look at Izzie, her face is pained once again. She may be a master manipulator, but that pain is real.

Distracted by their faces, I don't even realize I have

stopped until they both bring their focus back on one another.

Slowly, I bring myself to sit down as my eyes become captivated even further by the sight before me.

The tips of Izzie's red hair dangle at her hands, which are positioned below her shoulders as her naked body is on all fours, waiting for Liam.

"I said ass up." His voice is stern. She obeys.

Izzie's freckled face lowers to the mattress, which is draped in a single white sheet. Her pert ass is on display, and her toes wiggle in anticipation. My cock hardens as I take in this beautiful display. I bet her hair is soft and her skin smooth.

I picture her sitting cross-legged between my extended legs as I brush her hair after a day in the meadow. The smell of fresh daisies surrounds us as I take care of her.

A loud slap, skin to skin, brings me back.

Izzie is hissing with a red palm mark slowly making its way to the skin's surface. Liam walks around the bed and starts putting cuffs on her ankles, which are attached to restraints at each corner.

Raising my hand, I pull my hood down.

They are being vulnerable with me; this is giving it back in return.

Brushing my dark black hair out of my face, I continue to watch, still curious on how he plans to punish sweet Izzie.

Next, he grabs her wrists, locking them up the same

as her ankles. She will be unable to escape, at the mercy of her brother. Green eyes make contact with mine, biting her lip and the corner of her lips turns up. She loves this. Being on display. Played with and absolutely desired.

Liam is back at the foot of the bed, reaching forward, his fingers play with her folds, "Soaked." Looking over at me next, his brow raises, "Want a taste?" Then he extends his hand out to me. His finger is glistening with her, but I shake my head, rejecting the offer.

I hope it doesn't hurt her. I never want to hurt her.

"It's ok." Her voice trembles with need as she reassures me.

Liam is still looking me in the eye. Raising his finger to his lips, he slides it into his mouth. Hollowing his cheeks, he sucks. Tiny moans follow as he rolls his eyes to the back of his head. His other hand lays flat on his tattooed stomach and slowly moves up. Hooking his thumb under his white crop, he moves it up with his hand, exposing the rest of his chest.

My cock jerks against my pants; I can feel it dripping precum. Then he stops. Pulling his finger out, he drops his top and a low whimper breaks free from my vocal cords, catching me off guard. I freeze, shocked and panicked.

"You're right. She is enjoying this too much. And none of this is for her." Liam rasps and winks at me. Turning on his heel, his focus moves back to Izzie. He claps his hands together, "Shall we begin?"

LIAM

Izzie has been a very fucking bad girl. Telling my secrets without my consent. Such a naughty girl, pissing her brother off.

I want to punish her, choke her until she sees the stars, only to then let go and give her life back while my cock is buried deep inside.

And as appealing as the thought is, I can't. Not in front of Dex.

At first, the mute pissed me off. Along with his family. Moving here, possibly drawing attention to a space that didn't fucking need it. So I decided to rock his fucking world. But for the first time in my life, I felt bad about it. I felt bad that I hurt him and pissed my sister off.

That's why I can't play with her like that in front of him, even if she doesn't mind. It's our own game. It would only trigger more of his fucking demons, thanks to the sickening pedos in the basement. One who is rotting, the other smells of my piss.

Fuck. The fun we will have with him.

But now is not the time.

No. Because right now, it's time to punish the naked seductress restrained to my bed.

Going to my bedside table and pulling the door open, a selection of promiscuous toys are revealed. Dragging my fingers across them, I try to decide which one to start with.

Ah, yes. I choose you.

The cool metal feels good against my warm hands. Taking it out, I leave the drawer open and walk back to Izzie. Kneeling on the bed, I bend over and play with her dripping cunt once more. Her clit is swollen, begging to be sucked on. Gripping it between my fingers, I squeeze it once, causing her hips to buck, and I let go of her instantly and tsk, "This is not for you, sweet sister." Taking the cool metal clit clamp, I spread it apart and clamp it onto her sensitive nub. Sliding the loop up, I increase the squeeze against it; a sharp hiss follows. Her clit must be pounding as if there was a pulse inside of it. Her nerves are electrified with need.

Sitting up, I grip her ass next, spreading her cheeks apart to display her tight hole. My thumb circles it, and her hips wiggle as I allow a string of spit to leave my mouth and pool onto it. Izzie loves ass play. In her mind, she's anticipating my next move, shoving my finger deep inside of her. Not today.

Letting go of her ass, her cheeks cover the hole, which I also enjoy entertaining. Leaning over, I grab the wood paddle next and slap her hard with it. A loud crack fills the room from the wood connecting with her skin. I hit the same spot as I did with my hand earlier. Izzie's pussy reacts; her pelvis grinds against the bed in response.

I think not, sweet girl.

My own cock is hard as a rock, pushing against my pants to be freed.

Soon, I reassure him.

Next, I take my flogger and let the leather tassels skim across her skin. Moving from her spine, where goosebumps prick her skin, to the bottoms of her feet where her toes flex, trying not to react. Sensories are in overdrive.

"Does my sweet Izzie want to come?" I tease playfully.

Desperation drips off her words, "Please, Liam. I need to come. Touch me."

Placing my flogger down next to me, I undo my pants' button and lower my zipper. I know she can hear it. I know she thinks I am about to fuck her until she sees the stars.

Gripping my cock, I pull it out, and my thumb rubs my tip where precum is dripping. Spitting on my hard cock, I use my saliva as lube. Squeezing my tip causes my body to tingle, having Izzie at my mercy while my mute watches me play, goddamn.

"Naughty bitches don't come. They suffer," I rasp as I start working myself.

It starts slowly. A part of me wants to enjoy this. My hips thrust into my fist, and I watch as my abdomen flexes with each movement. I can't take it. Working myself faster, I squeeze my cock even harder, chasing my orgasm, which is building.

My breathing gets heavier. Izzie wiggles under me, teasing and taunting. Fucking bitch. My forearm aches; I'm not used to hand-fucking myself; usually Izzie handles me. It's been a while since she has last been this naughty. Then my balls tighten as the familiar tingle builds. Working myself as fast as I can, ropes of my warm come begin to explode out of my cock.

"Fucking take it. You naughty little bitch." My voice is hoarse.

"Decorate me."

Her response pisses me off. She's supposed to be suffering for telling our secrets.

Coming all over her back. My white release coats her pale skin. My spine tingles, and it goes all the way to the tip of my toes. I don't let up until every fucking drop is drained from my balls. The steady stream becomes more sporadic. Shaking my semi-hard cock, the last drops land on her ass. Bending down, I stick my tongue out and taste myself on her, mixed together, my tastebuds ignite. We are delicious. I then reach down and pull the clit clamp off Izzie; she moans into the mattress.

Sitting up, I shove my cock back in my pants and turn around; my chest is panting as I look over to Dex. He liked it. Watching. I can tell by his hard cock and hooded eyes looking back at me.

Once he realizes I'm staring, he abruptly rises to his feet. Stumbling at first as he steps forward. As he catches his balance, he rushes out of the room. His feet pound down each step on the stairs. And just like that, he is gone.

CHAPTER 14
DEX

This isn't okay. I need to get home. I need to get to mama.

Throwing my hood back up over my head, I dash through the meadow into the trees. My cock is no longer hard, but the ache still lingers. This needs to stop. Mama has never seen me like this; I can't go home like this. What the fuck was I thinking? The night sky is dark; stars shine through the branches above, lighting my path. I stop suddenly, out of breath, placing both hands on the thick tree trunk bent over as I gather my thoughts.

Why did I like that?

Turning around, I let my back slide down the trunk. My knees stay bent at my chest with my arms crossed over them and my head resting on top. As my lip quivers, tears slide down my dry cheek.

Why did I fucking like that?

My cock has never voluntarily gotten hard before. When it began pressing against my pants while sitting in the chair watching Izzie lay naked on display, I was so fucking scared. Then Liam took his cock out, and I was captivated. His strong hand wrapped around his thick girth, working himself fast and hard. I wanted nothing more than to take my own cock out and join him.

Finally, for the first time, I think I felt normal?

Izzie, I will always feel the need to watch over and protect. Something about her will always draw me to her. Liam though, he has shown me how to live without being in constant pain. He takes my mind off it, allowing me to feel what pleasure could be like. At first, he scared me. He was a threat to me and my family. Liam could have told people he knew where we were and turned us in without a bat of an eye, but he didn't. Don't get me wrong, he was mean and vindictive. But Izzie protected me; she comforted me. Knowing it would be impossible to return it all.

The life I have experienced in the past couple weeks is brand new and exciting; could it be clouding my judgment?

Loud grunts leave my throat. My mind battles with itself.

All I want is some fucking clarity.

Sniffling my nose, tears continue down my face.

I wish we could go back to when mama surprised me with Izzie in the cellar. I would have taken such good care of her. She would have been happy with me there, I'm sure of it. Regular meals, walks in the meadow, and comfort in sitting in silence with one another. None of this confusion and confliction would have existed.

A twig cracks, catching my attention. Something is coming towards me.

"It's just me, buddy."

Jasper.

How did he know I was here?

I don't turn to look at him; I can't.

"I heard you while walking back to the barn. Something felt off, so I figured I would come check on you."

Jasp kneels next to me; I can feel his knee graze against my elbow. He blows out a deep sigh. It's bad news, I can feel it. "It's true. I'm so sorry, Dex." Jasper pauses, allowing me to absorb what he just said. "After we burnt Sutton down, a massive manhunt ensued. They dug deep into all of us. The Ryan's officially adopted you. They left out the part as to why. Just that your birth parents were junkies. I haven't told Ris yet."

Once he finishes speaking, we sit together in silence. I digest the truth. The truth I always knew was real.

"She is going to let it rain blood, murder, and mayhem if she finds out the Walters are still alive." Jasper chuckles; I'm sure he is picturing mama in her natural habitat, covered in blood and smiling like a fucking maniac.

Looking up, I wipe my eyes with the back of my hand.

"I'll wait until morning. Don't take off before then;

she'll need to make sure you're ok." His ask isn't a big one; I accept it easily. Going to stand, his words stop me. "You are ok, right? I'm here for you, Dex. You are family."

Swallowing the lump in my throat, I reach my hand out and rub his shoulder in reassurance. I wasn't okay; I'm still not. It's so much to process, and even more confusion has arisen since. But I won't let my past fucking define me.

Laying in bed, my eyes stare at the grooves in each piece of wood. The sun is shining through the cracks; it's morning, and sleep has escaped me. The longer I have laid here with the truth, the more I have come to terms with how much knowing for certain hits differently. It has changed nothing. No weight has been lifted off of me. My mind tried to go down the why me path, but I blocked it, suppressed it. Anxiety attempted to build in my chest as my eyes squeezed shut as I tried to force my brain to remember my time with the Walters. All attempts failed.

My sole purpose in life was to be used and abused.

I just need to fucking accept it. I was strategically placed in that room for *her*.

And love, it never existed until I met my true family, the Ashfords.

My bed dips.

Mama.

"Jasp told me. I have him seeing if there are any records of them still being alive. If they are... a family vacation could be in order," Mama says giddily, bouncing on the mattress on her knees. She hasn't killed in ages. Blood is a kink of hers and Jaspers; she is definitely getting off on the thought of hurting people who hurt me.

"I'll shove a broken bottle up her cunt. Make her really feel, no matter how high. Then, what about if I shove the same bottle down his throat? The Walters, we are the Ashfords; it's a pleasure." A hysterical laugh escapes her. "The Walters are so fucked. They have no idea what the Queen and King of Sutton are truly capable of. Sutton was just a taste of the party we can throw."

Rolling to my side, I take her in, her dark, long hair and her pouty lips. Eyes that are completely dilated as she pictures everything that she is saying. Mama is beautiful.

Placing my hand in hers, "Mama," is all I can say while shaking my head. Her free hand reaches to my forehead, moving my hair to the side, "You don't want to come?" Her brows raise questioning.

"You can stay here. We will go if someone hasn't gotten to them before us. They better not have. Those fuckers are mine." Mama is getting excited again. I smile in response.

This is what family looks like.

Her fingers continue to play with my hair; it's soothing, calming my mind. My eyelids feel like weights are hanging from them as they close. Sleep finally overcomes me.

Shut up, shut up, shut up.

A loud gasp wakes me. Sitting up in my bed, sweat is coating my body, and I can hear my heart beating in my ears.

Looking around, mama is no longer lying next to me.

The gasp came from me. I scared myself awake.

Blinking several times, I try to remember what it was I was dreaming about. Was it a memory that my brain is trying to protect me from? Why can't I fucking remember?

Swinging my legs over the edge of my bed, my feet pad on the wood floor and lead me out to the loft railing. My hands grip the wood; looking around, the barn is empty. I am alone.

Rushing back into my room, I slide my shorts on, throw my sweater over my head, slide my shoes on, and haul it downstairs.

Hitting my head, I need to remember. What was I dreaming? Why did I wake up suppressing it?

A furious yell erupts from my lungs as a white piece

of paper attached to the barn door catches my attention; it changes my focus, if only for a short time.

A note.

Mama left a lamp on, which helps me read it; *family vacation* is crossed out, and under it is '*Couples Retreat*'.

They have a lead. I'd be shocked if they found the junkies alive, truthfully. I don't want to get excited over nothing, because that's what this all could be. Nothing.

Sliding the heavy wood door open, darkness welcomes me. I slept the entire day away. Panic still lingers; my anxiety has been the worst it's ever been lately. Everything happening around me is related to me, and I have no fucking control over any of it.

At Sutton, most things were predictable; we made the rules. Sure, we would spend time locked away for being bad, but we always saw it coming. Lately, nothing is as it seems. Everything's a surprise. The one constant I had, watching Izzie in the meadow from the shadows, is even destroyed. Unsure of what to do, I close the barn door and lock it with the padlock. Once our home is secure, I take off, running deep into the woods. My hideaway. My safe place.

Getting lost in my thoughts, loud bangs bring me back to the present. How did I get here?

I'm not ok.

Izzie opens the door. Her initial reaction is to reach forward, to comfort me, but I step back.

"No, no, no," I barely whisper, in pain. A silent scream tries to leave my open mouth as Liam rushes past

Izzie. His strong arms embrace me into a hug. His musky scent is comforting as I allow his touch. I relax into him. Liam tries to calm me with long shushing and rubbing my back with tiny circles. His cheek brushes against mine, and I lean into him even further.

"I got you, my beautiful broken boy."

CHAPTER 15
DEX

My obsession started with Izzie. Now, both of them are who I run to if mama and Jasp aren't around. I didn't even think twice about it.

Normally, I would sit and shake alone. Trying to make the thoughts disappear until I passed out from exhaustion. This time, my instincts said go to *them,* and I did. A calmness washes over me as Liam holds me steady in his arms. His scent, musky, comforts as he whispers, "What happened, broken boy?"

My head shakes *no* in response. I don't remember my dream, only that it scared the shit out of me. Sometimes my brain does this, blacking out things that are triggering in my subconscious to help protect me.

A crack of thunder startles me. Letting go of Liam, I jump back. Izzie is standing beside him with worry riddling her face. She is unsure of what to do.

"Let's get inside before it starts raining." She suggests, so I nod and follow them both inside.

Bypassing the kitchen, we go straight up the stairs and go into Liam's room. I find the familiar chair from last time and curl myself up onto it.

I can feel two sets of eyes on me, but I can't bring myself to look up at either of them. My hood covers the top half of my face, where I continue to hide.

"What happened?" Izzie blurts out, breaking the mounting tension. I don't respond, still cowering here in the corner. Perhaps with time I'll know what exactly happened while I slept and my mind spoke.

Rain begins to hit the glass window.

Tick Tock.

She's coming. Get ready, Dex. Maybe tonight won't be so bad.

Shut up, shut up, shut up.

Fucking suppress already.

Another crack of thunder sends shivers up my spine.

The creek of the floorboard causes me to squeeze my eyes shut.

She's here. The more you fight it, the worse it will be.

Hitting the side of my head, I just want it to stop. Why won't it fucking stop?

Hands touch my knees and I smell musk; it's Liam.

"Broken boy. What can I do?"

His presence helps. Just like mama's. He is safe; he isn't going to hurt me or us, my family. Needing to distract myself, I look up at him. His hair is disheveled, beautiful dark eyes with long lashes look back at me, and his chiseled jawline with thin lips begs for my thumb to rub against them. Liam is wearing a distressed white tee crop this time, torn and marked up with black felt marker. His legs are bare, with only a pair of underwear on. Some raised scarring can be seen from what his dad did. My eyes try to analyze each one; they want to memorize the ridges and divots.

"Hey, focus on me. Only me. Ok?" His voice is my strength.

Taking his hand into mine, electricity flows through him to me. My chest warms.

Tears swell in my eyes. I am so fucking confused, but this here feels so good. I flip his palm over so it is face up. Reaching my finger out, I speak to him the only way I can. Another spark moves through my fingertip once I touch his skin. After I have settled from the second jolt, I start tracing. Starting with a W, Liam stays quiet as he watches me. H is next, then Y. His face frowns, confused. I then spell out the rest of my question. As I went on, his face changed from frowning to biting his lip while nodding his head.

Liam softly asks, "Can Izzie know your question?"

I give one curt nod, and he repeats my question out loud, "He asked, why did dad hurt me?"

Because I need to understand. Something in this life needs to make sense to me. Anything.

Rain is still hitting the windows; it's all I hear as I wait for a response.

Blowing out a deep breath, Liam rakes his fingers through his hair and starts talking, "You know how they say abuse is a cycle? It won't be broken until you break it? Well, his dad did it to him, to discipline. Then taught him how to do it to others and himself. He taught him just how deep to cut so they wouldn't bleed out by accidentally hitting an artery. How to make the most perfect and imperfect scars. I think he eventually started seeing it as art and he liked it. Like, really fucking liked it because he went off and became a surgeon, where he could cut all fucking day long. But that wasn't good enough. No. He then had to come home and do it to me, too. It was worse when I was bad or disobeyed the good doctor. Izzie avoided it because she learnt quickly how to cater to his ego. I was more stubborn. And now, I do it too. But worse."

My heart drops into the depths of my stomach hearing his story. And when he spoke about himself being worse, he spoke with such shame and disgust in himself. Now I am the one wanting; no, I am needing to comfort him. My hand reaches out, but I stop myself. I need to know one more thing before I take this leap.

Taking his palm back in my hand, I continue writing rapidly. I hope he catches all the letters I'm writing, H then O and W. His eyes follow the movement of my finger, focusing only on me. Raising my finger off his skin as I finish the last word, I wait for Liam's reply.

Clearing his throat, he looks up at me as he speaks, "You can trust me. You can trust Izzie. You won't ever be the next person on my table; I can fucking promise you that. If we wanted you dead, you would be. If we didn't want you here, you wouldn't be. Shit started out bad, I will admit that. Your mama stole my fucking sister. Then you broke in, and I casually told you about your past. I felt bad the minute it came out of my mouth. The look not only on your face, but Izzie's killed me. But know this; my past defines me. No one can argue that otherwise. But yours doesn't. What happened to you was really fucking shitty, but you are not that person. And just think, if none of that stuff happened to either of us, you wouldn't be here right now in this moment with us. Your mama wouldn't have stolen Izzie, and I would have never showed up to the barn that day banging on the door." He pauses while keeping eye contact with me. His dark eyes are pleading with me to believe him, and I do.

Cupping my face, he continues, "Our pasts lead us here, to each other for a reason, Dex. You can trust us. Just like we can trust you and your family. No matter how fucking crazy they are." He chuckles at the end, but still he is sincere in his words.

My hand gently touches his, which is still embracing me. My mind is free of the fear from the rain and my nightmare. For the first time in forever, I am solely immersed in this moment right here, right now.

I believe them.

CHAPTER 16
LIAM

Bringing my face closer to his, I can feel his warm breath dancing on my skin. Goosebumps start to coat my body. Moving slowly, I inch forward. Dex doesn't stop me, nor does he move toward me. I don't want to spook him, so I continue taking each movement at the same pace so he has time to absorb what is going to occur. My lips against his; it's inevitable, it always has been before we both ever knew it.

"Whenever the bad thoughts come, I want you to picture this moment. Make right now what you see instead of *that*. Make my touch what you feel, my palm against your soft skin. Next time it rains, always see tonight." My voice rasps.

I should take my own advice, but it is easier said than done, and frankly, my broken boy needs this more than I do. There is light within my darkness, but I don't know if he has the same luxury.

He seems shocked when I mention the rain, but it doesn't take rocket science to notice how he's reacted to it tonight; it's triggering. And from what I read in his file, it was raining that night and the night Iris found him. He was torturing himself by sitting outside in it, at Sutton. Fresh from being sentenced and confused about what he had just done, fuck. Shaking my own head to get rid of the thought, I can't wait any longer; I need his lips on mine.

Focusing my eyes on his lips, the distinct cupids bow to his plump bottom, I remove all space between us and softly place my lips on his. Breathing through his nose, he takes in a deep breath; his body becomes stiff, unsure how to react. I pull back slightly, then go back for more, giving Dex many long, soft, intimate kisses. Like when our skin touched for the first time, the electric current moves between our lips. My forehead rests against his as our kiss breaks for the last time. Our lashes brush against each other, getting tangled as we absorb this monumental moment. He let me in.

Both our breathing has picked up; I rub his nose with mine, and I have completely forgotten my sister is here, on my bed, watching us, until she lets out a tiny sneeze behind me.

Izzie uses the moment to ask, "Can I stay? Can I watch?" Her voice is hungry and full of desire.

Looking at Dex, I wait for him to give me a signal; this is his show, not ours. Closing his eyes, his breath evens out. My hands are still on his face, with his hands embracing them. His thumb rubbing circles on the back of my hand, then one curt nod occurs, and that's all we need.

I relay the message to Izzie, "Yes. You can stay."

Leaning back, the lost connection of our skin hurts, and I let go of his beautiful face. Looking down his body, I see a bulge in his pants, he is erect. Moving my eyes back to his, his face has morphed from pleasure to shame. Not on my fucking watch.

"Can I suck you?"

My broken boy's face pains. I need to bring him back, "Remember Dex, me, this moment. Focus on it." A small groan comes from him; he's trying.

Taking my hands, I rub the top of his thighs, "Focus on this, Dex." I continue to encourage. His eyes open as he nods, watching my hands move, which only causes his cock to grow harder. Taking one of my hands, he flips my palm over and speaks, writing on it.

Yes.

My mouth waters the second he gives me permission. Instinct tries to take over, but my mind is able to slow it down. This cannot be rushed with him, not yet. He needs to see how pleasure isn't always pain, like he has only ever known it. Pleasure can be euphoric, liberating, and soul-binding. And he is letting me, the one who was a complete dick to him at first, show him that. I cannot let him down.

Undoing his pants button, his zipper follows, and I pull it down. A loud crack of thunder makes us both jump. Keeping my eyes on him, I wait before continuing and let him calm down. A few moments pass; his finger taps my forearm, encouraging me to continue and I do. Once the zipper is fully undone, I grip his waistband and begin pulling his pants down. Dex lifts his hips, allowing me to take them further down his legs. I bring his underwear with them, and once I pass his pelvis, his large, hard cock springs out, bouncing off his covered stomach with precum leaking out of his tip. Biting my lip, I hiss, "Fuck."

Before I get distracted, I pull his pants down to his ankles. Tapping his foot, I signal for Dex to lift them up and he does, allowing me to completely free him of any restrictions. Tossing them next to us, I then place my hands on his knees and spread his legs as far apart as I can while he sits back in the chair.

He groans as I move my hands up further on his bare tights. I can see his hands are clenched into fists at his side. He's scared, but he trusts me.

"I promise it won't hurt." I reassure him.

I continue teasing him; my fingers brush over his trimmed pubes, and I twist a few around my finger, prolonging the anticipation. The longer the foreplay, the better the release, but my broken boy doesn't know that yet. I won't toy with him long; I'll need to build him up to it with time.

My mouth is inches away from his cock. Opening my mouth, I let saliva drip down onto his sensitive tip. He hisses, and his hips rock ever so slightly from the sensation.

"At any time, if you need me to stop, tap my arm and I will." I whisper to him as my mouth hovers over his cock; my eyes look up at him and he nods, telling me he understands. Then I notice his own eyes are hooded, which tells me he is feeling pleasure, even if it's just a tiny bit.

Wrapping my lips around him, I allow my tongue to rub along his slit and his hips buck once again, which only pushes him further into my mouth. But it isn't enough; I need him down my fucking throat.

Moving my mouth further down his shaft, his cock leaks onto my tongue, and delicious salty precum drips on my tongue and taste buds. Hollowing out my cheeks, I breathe heavily through my nose as I take him deeper. Reaching the back of my throat, I inch him a bit further as I gag, but I don't let that stop me. Drool is dripping down my chin as I start working him, moving my mouth up and down his cock, allowing his tip to rub against my tonsils. I have one goal, and it is to make him fucking cum. My fingers grip his thighs harder as I work him vigorously; my fingernails dig into his skin, causing him to hiss. For a moment I think I have taken it too far and wait for his tap, but nothing comes, which is relief.

More faint groans follow the hiss; my broken boy's hips start moving on their own, he is no longer in control. No, Dex's sex drive is, and it is chasing the orgasm that is building inside of his body.

Removing my hands from his thighs, I grip his base and bring his cock out of my throat, but not out of my mouth. My lips stay wrapped around him, and my tongue teases. Dex's hands move, unsure of where to put them or what to do. I'll have to teach him that gripping my hair is ok, but that can be for another day. I squeeze him as his cock swells; any second now it's going to hit. Just as I think that, his cock erupts. Warm cum coats my tongue, but I don't let up; I want to get every last fucking drop out of him.

Izzie moans, and I can hear the bed squeak behind me as she rides her fingers. My own dick gets even harder in my pants; between Dex and Izzie I am overstimulated and desperate for my balls to be released of all the built-up sexual frustration. But this isn't about me tonight. So, I don't let that distract me as I continue sucking Dex's cock.

I cannot get enough; I need more. Taking him deep once more, I work him harder and faster. More ropes of cum shoot out inside of me. The drool dripping down my chin is now also mixed with his creamy white release. I can feel his legs trembling against my body, opening my eyes, I look up at him. Dex has his mouth open as his chest heaves. His eyes are focused on what my mouth is doing; he is entranced.

Pulling back, my tongue slowly licks the underside of his dick, which is starting to soften as I continue to milk him. A shiver washes over Dex, and his back arches off the chair.

Fuck, I wish someone would grab my hair, pull it hard and tell me how fucking great they feel. Perhaps one day he will, but not today. Izzie will show him and teach him what is okay.

As I bring his cock past my lips, my tongue twirls on his tip once more before we fully disconnect. His head falls back as his orgasm subsides.

I lick my lips and smile, "Fucking delicious, broken boy." I need him to know this is safe pleasure, good pleasure. And it's the truth, he tasted exquisite, a delicacy.

"That was so fucking hot." Izzie pants behind me. A faint smile forms on Dex's mouth, but his eyes stay closed. I don't wipe my face; I want to feel him dry on my chin so I can feel him with me all night.

My own heart is racing; sweat is beading at my hairline. Gripping my shirt, I throw it off, exposing my torso in an effort to cool down. I then grab Dex's pants and help put them back on while he is sedated. Kindness after pleasure is just as important; I need him to see that. Aftercare.

I get to his hips; he lifts them slightly so I can bring them up, covering his cock so he can feel covered and safe. I would throw a blanket on him too, but it's way too fucking hot for that shit.

Standing up, I cup my cock and squeeze it. Not now buddy, maybe Izzie will help us out in the morning. I chuckle to myself. It's not maybe, she fucking will.

"Dex, will you sleep in bed with us?" Izzie asks him sweetly. Before he is able to respond, I interject, "Baby steps, sister. I did just suck his cock. He needs to be eased into all of this. It's new."

Pushing his hair back as his eyes give into sleep, I continue, "See Dex, it's pleasure too. Not just pain, baby."

Kissing his forehead, I breathe him in once more before stepping back. He's out, and I am not far behind him. Jumping into bed with my sister, the second my head hits that pillow, my heavy eyes close, sending me into the deepest sleep I have had in fucking years.

CHAPTER 17
IZZIE

Watching Liam with Dex last night, it was different than how he is with me—rough and unapologetic. Just how we like it. With Dex, he is soft, gentle, and perhaps at times even submissive?

He may never be mine, but he is ours.

Shit.

Iris is going to kick my ass over this. I chuckle to myself at the thought.

"Izzie, on my cock. Now," Liam barks; his eyes aren't even open. Fucker must have heard my snicker.

I don't move immediately; Liam growls through his teeth, and it makes my pussy tingle. I like when he is needy for me with a side of asshole. It makes the sex rough and intense. The thin sheet covers my bare body, with the exception of my panties. Stretching my arms above my head, I let out a loud yawn, only to further taunt Liam. He won't like that. And just as predicted and right on queue, Liam throws the sheet off me, and with his strong arms, reaches over my waist and hooks underneath me. His other free hand grips the other side, and he lifts me up, turns me around and sits me on top of his hard cock.

He's bare; the shaft of his cock is pressed between my cheeks. I grind my hips slowly in a circle and tease him mercilessly. Liam's eyes are hooded while a loud hiss pierces the quiet space. Biting my lip, I don't let up. This is too much fucking fun, "Hmmm, does my bad boy like that? Should I keep going until you cum all over my ass?" Reaching ahead of me, my small fingers grip his face, "Or would you prefer coming inside of me?" My voice is husky with seduction, playing his own game back at him.

His hands squeeze my hips hard and pride rushes through me; I am getting to him. Leaning forward, with my hand still tightly gripping his face, my teeth nip at his bottom lip, pulling it just far enough before letting it go. He is prompt to lick the same spot, and as he does, I take the tip of my tongue and trail it up his lips; my tongue brushes roughly against his in an effort to keep my control. He allows it. Liam is intrigued, where and how far am I going to take this?

I let go of him and place my hands on his bare tattooed chest. My nails dig into his flesh, and steadily I drag them down as I lean back, inch by inch, taking it as slow as I possibly can. Liam's hips buck; pain is his pleasure, as it is mine. But only good pain, such as this.

He is getting anxious, impatient, and needy. Just how I like him.

Taking his hands off my skin, he rapidly moves to rid me of my panties. Liam grabs ahold of the hem and tears them on each side of my hips. He then grabs at the fabric now laying on top of his pelvis, where mine is exposed, and roughly slides the fabric out from under me.

The discomfort causes me to rock up slightly; he takes advantage of my momentary lapse in judgment by throwing my torn panties to the side, then lifting me up and dropping me on top of his cock; it impales me in one go. My pussy is dripping and acting in replacement of lube. A loud moan flies out of me, not thinking, as Dex is still asleep in the chair.

Liam can read my face and smirks, "You want him to see you like this, don't you? Show him that you own me, if not more than he ever could?"

I can be a conniving bitch, but not with Dex. Not once has that thought or jealousy crossed my mind. The more I get to know him, the more I need to protect and care for him.

Shaking my head, I whisper sincerely, "Never."

All movements stop for a brief moment as Liam looks back at me, taking in my absolute honesty. A quick, subtle nod is all it takes; he believes me. There has never been a reason for him not to, but I'm sure he wasn't expecting such an answer.

Placing my hands on the chest I just marred; no blood was drawn, but I can feel the scratches with pride. Grinding my pussy against him, my clit never wants me to stop, and his cock is working my g-spot. My long red hair hangs over my shoulders as we both fuck each other, panting and admiring each other. As my toes begin to tingle, Liam reaches up and grasps my throat. Beads of sweat start to adorn my face the harder we go. I am unable to catch a full breath; it only amplifies the sensation flowing throughout my body.

Throwing my head back, I catch sight of Dex, who is still in the corner on the chair, but is now awake. Squeezing my tits, my back arches as my orgasm washes over me. Sweat is dripping off me, and Liam squeezes my throat tighter.

"It's okay, Dex. I like it like this." I groan breathlessly in reassurance; I don't want him to be frightened.

His eyes stay on us, and I continue to ride Liam's cock through my orgasm. My pussy walls grip him tightly. It doesn't take long for me to feel his cum coating the inside of me.

"Dexy, this is how our sweet girl likes it. Filthy fucking whore, aren't you sister? Show Dexy just how filthy you are." Liam's smile is sinister and I eat it up.

Crashing my lips into his, it's chaos. Our teeth clash and our tongues dance for dominance in a game in which neither of us will win fully. He nips at my lip; it stings, and I pull back slightly. "Pussy," he mumbles, followed by a cheeky wink.

Bastard.

Our movements slow down, but our hearts beat

rapidly. A couple aftershocks cause my body to tremble, leaving me completely at his mercy. Letting go of my throat, he moves to my nipples, taking them between his fingers and tugging them hard. Liam's fingernails embed themselves inside the sensitive skin, and I flinch at the sensation.

"Go shower. We have things to do today." Liam instructs before letting go of me.

Instinct takes over, and I slap his chest, "Fucking prick." I can feel my face frowning at him. Throwing his head back, he starts laughing hysterically. What a fucking psychopath.

"You love this prick; remember that."

Rolling my eyes, I blow out a sigh, "Yeah, and I don't understand why sometimes."

I slide off him, not because he instructed, but because I am over it. Our cum drips out of me, and I let it paint him by pushing it out harder. His eyes are concentrated on what I am doing; he fucking loves it and begins rubbing it into his skin like moisturizer.

As I finish, I look over to our guest, who has a massive bulge under his pants, "Good morning, Dex; hope you slept well." I wink while jumping off the bed. I don't wait for a reaction from either boy and swiftly make my exit.

LIAM

"There's good pain and bad pain. That was good pain. You never have to worry about the bad pain with me. I'll always be gentle, unless you ask otherwise." The words leave my mouth without any thought. It's automatic. A side I never knew myself to possess.

Dex, my mute, is the only one to bring this side out in me.

He doesn't respond. I watch his eyes take me in, roaming my body as I lay here, freshly fucked and naked.

Strands of dark hair are stuck to my forehead even as I roll to reach a joint from the bedside table. Placing it between my lips, I light it and take a long first hit. Getting high after sex is the best feeling. It amplifies the afterglow.

Standing up, I get an idea. My feet pad against the chilled hardwood; the heat has yet to invade the house. Snatching my knife off the desk, I start scratching out the words floating before me onto the minimal space left on my bedroom wall.

Chaos and Fire
Calmness and Water
Balance has entered my soul

Everything is going to change; it has already started. The weed is either hiding the anxiety of it or I truly am content; no, that's the wrong word; I am accepting it. Not fighting it, and neither is Izzie.

Looking over to Dex, who is still propped on the chair, I take another hit and blow it out in his direction before asking, "Do you feel remorse? For any of it, ever?" He shakes his head no in response.

Relief washes over me; neither do I.

Walking over to Dex, still naked, I look at his lap and notice his erection, but I don't say anything, baby steps. Instead, I climb onto his lap with my back resting against the armrest and my legs hanging over the edge. With my joint hanging out of my mouth, another thought rolls over me, "Have you missed it? Hurting people?"

He looks at me, confused. Lifting his hand, Dex uses the tip of his finger to trace along my inked torso. *I only want to hurt those who hurt me or my family.*

"We need to get you a notebook, baby." I chuckle. Because I know if I were super high, there would be no way I could decipher this shit.

Dex throws his head back, smiling at my comment. Fuck, it feels good knowing I put that smile on his face.

"If *we* ever do anything that hurts you. Do it, Dex. Make us pay for it."

Raising his head back up, he looks me in the eye and nods.

Then, out of nowhere, I blurt, "You know... you're changing me too... even Izzie."

Time stops; the room is a blur faded in the background. The only thing that matters is in focus, the two of us.

"I drive out of state. Small towns with shitty cops and no resources are primarily where I go. Once I have my target, I hunt them, then bring them back. Bonus points if they are dicks. But my appetite doesn't discriminate. It's so remote and isolated out here, as you know. Sometimes I do it in the backyard, easy to clean up, or the basement like the Ryan's."

Izzie has seen what I do, but to say it out loud to someone other than her, is different, uncomfortable even. But to make one thing clear, I'm not ashamed. Since my dad, I crave it. Interrupting us is my stomach, which has started to make distress calls of hunger, followed by Izzie, who pokes her head in, "Breakfast?"

CHAPTER 18
DEX

A few days have passed.

After watching Liam eat eggs, toast, and human flesh for breakfast, I decided I could never be a cannibal. Even the pancakes Izzie made were hard to get down at the sight, but it's something I have to get used to, too.

The three of us went for a walk after checking on the barn; mama and Jasp were still on their retreat. I'll have to go back again today or tomorrow to make sure everything is the way it should be. Left alone.

Opening the fridge door, I keep forgetting the heads are still in here, for whatever reason. They have been drained for a while; why hasn't he done anything with them? The blood in the containers makes me cringe. Does he drink this? Unknowingly, my body has bent over, and I am inches away from some old lady's decapitated head. My arm is resting on the top of the fridge door and as I go to stand, Liam's voice startles me; I didn't even hear him coming up behind me.

"I add gelatin to one, let it sit for a couple hours, then eat it as a snack. The other one, I need to freeze; I use it to make stew gravy or combine in a marinade, depending on the day's menu. And the heads, if I'm in the mood, I'll crack their skulls open like a coconut and eat their brains like ramen." He finishes explaining cheerfully.

Turning around, I look at him, shocked; his hair is a mess as per usual while he is wearing white tight jeans that hug all the right places, black combat boots, and his signature white crop. Walking over to him, I swing the fridge door closed behind me and lean forward, brushing my lips softly against his. Liam's breath hitches, not expecting it. And honestly, I didn't either. But I want to show him it doesn't bother me. I hear him inhale deeply; his cock hardens against mine; he is only an inch or two taller than me.

Without warning, his hands cup my cheeks, and he begins to devour me. I've never kissed like this before; my body stiffens, unsure of what to do. Liam's tongue pushes itself through my lips, and mine meets him, instinct kicks in. My heart races from nerves and excitement. Raising my hands, they fall on top of his; I never want them to leave me. Battling for dominance, our tongues dance with one another. Our saliva builds in my mouth; swallowing, I relax further into him. Never have I allowed a person this close to me. Now I have a part of him inside of me, and I need fucking more.

The sound of petite feet catches my attention, Izzie. I can feel she's close. "Hmm, boys, and here I thought we were going to check on the barn." Her voice is full of lust. Opening one eye to squint, her beautiful pale frame is decorated in a yellow sundress with her flowy red hair hanging over her shoulders. With spread legs, her one hand has gone missing underneath the thin fabric. Liam notices my distraction and pulls back; our lips disconnect, and I miss it; I wasn't done yet. With his hands still securely on my face, he looks over to where I am looking and tsks at his horny sister, "Thanks for reminding us." Izzie's face frowns; she blows out a huff of annoyance, "Pussy teases, both of you."

Izzie pouts and jumps off the counter. I smile at her, and she winks back.

Conflict enters my head; I just want to let her in. To let her touch me, to get even closer to her, to stand between her legs while she sits on the counter, but I fucking can't. Letting go of Liam's hands, my fists ball up, and I fall back into a familiar habit, hitting my head to forget, to punish. I only get one punch in before Liam stops me, wrapping his hands around my wrist.

"Come back to me. Focus on me. Whatever it is, it's ok. Focus on that night, that moment, my touch. I'm here. You are here. My beautiful, broken boy." He's scared. Worried. Comforting. Closing my eyes, I focus on his touch. His hands against my skin. His mouth sucking my cock. Pleasure isn't always pain.

Baby steps.

One day, I fucking hope, I can let her in like I have let him.

Something cool runs down my cheek, opening my eyes, Liam's thumb is brushing the same spot, "It's okay to cry. I got you. Just like I got Izzie." He reassures me, then licks the tear away with his tongue.

"Dex? After we check on the barn, maybe we can hang out in the meadow for a bit? I know how much we like it there."

Nodding my head, I do miss sitting there in the treeline and watching her for hours.

"Then let's go, baby." Liam kisses my nose then intertwines my fingers with his; using his other hand, he reaches over and slaps Izzie's ass hard. I can hear her skin crack as she looks back at him, smiling. That's good pain, the kind she told me she likes. So it doesn't trigger me.

Before we walk out the door, I stop, let go of Liam, and pull my sweater off over my head, throwing it to the ground. I catch both their eyes looking at me in shock. I've not exposed myself like this in a very long time, unless at home with mama and Jasp. I'm standing here in the kitchen, with heads in the fridge, showing my own skin, with a black tee covering my torso.

"Thank you, Dex," Izzie whispers in shock. Liam follows, "My brave, broken boy."

Liam was right.

Things are changing.

The sun shines down on Izzie from high in the clear blue sky. A slight breeze remains throughout our time here, in the meadow, where it all began. And for the first time, I can feel it brush across my bare arms from my spot, sitting against my tree.

Liam is here next to me; his arm will brush against mine from time to time, shivers and goosebumps briefly appear each time. Everything about this is new and terrifying, but they are trusting me, and I need to show it back that I am trusting them. I am consciously doing my best to not self-sabotage, to ensure I don't get spooked and climb back into my protective shell.

Mama would be so proud if she saw this.

I miss her. We have never been apart unless it was forced at Sutton. But a part of her must know Liam and Izzie are safe; she wouldn't have left otherwise. She is allowing me to grow while she keeps her distance, to not interfere or hinder.

This has to be so fucking hard on her. Because I know at times, this has been really hard on me. Jasp has been great too. I'm sure he has helped keep her mind distracted.

Thinking back on everything, I feel like I want a love like that. Where you would die for one another and live. To match each other's crazy highs and support during the dark lows.

I never thought I deserved a life or love like that outside of the Ashfords. Not because of anything they did, but because of the Ryans and *her*.

"Thank you for letting us in. I know I was dick before, but your mama did steal my sister, and I didn't want attention coming on this part of the woods... for obvious reasons." Liam explains, his tone is apologetic, which only lasts a moment before changing to defensive and serious. "Don't tell Izzie I'm soft; I'll fuck you so hard you won't be able to walk properly for weeks if you do." His threat is hollow, I think?

Looking toward him, a devilish glint beams off his eyes; perhaps it's not.

Smirking back at him, I try to suppress a nervous giggle, but it doesn't work. My hand covers my mouth in an effort to muffle it, but Liam grabs ahold of my wrist to stop me. My body stiffens nervously.

"Your laugh is beautiful, broken boy." He praises sweetly.

I relax into his hold, following the compliment as he continues, "Don't worry, I won't fuck you until you give me permission."

Liam's reassurance is everything. He is nothing like *her*.

Our fingers intertwine, and I work up the nerve to trace circles against the back of his hand with my thumb. Liam doesn't stop me. At the same time, my eyes linger on Izzie, who is still filling her basket with fresh wild flowers. Bright pinks, blues, and yellows are hanging out of the brown wicker. They are almost as beautiful as her. But nothing can truly compare.

We checked on the barn; mama and Jasp are still

away. Only the devil knows the kind of shit they are getting up to right now. And I bet mama is having the best time doing it.

Another chuckle escapes before I can stop it at the thought. My eyes shift to Liam, who is squeezing my hand in reassurance, whose face also has a wide grin adorning it.

I've gone from having ironclad control over myself to casually laughing. This is fucking insane. Surreal, actually. How is this my life?

He must sense I am back inside of my head. Shifting his body towards mine, attempting to change the subject, "I think it's time, baby."

My eyes squint, unsure of what he is referencing.

"Tonight. Your dad. It's been days since we left him downstairs with his rotting whore of a wife. I haven't fed him or given him any water. We need to do it before his body gives up." Liam explains softly.

I'm ready. I know I am. This chapter of my life is ready to be over. I fucking need it to be over.

It's time.

CHAPTER 19
LIAM

Relief and pain.

My broken boy is conflicted. Battling another war in his brain.

All conflict will be resolved soon.

He will end that barely alive motherfucker rotting in my basement, stewing away in his own piss and shit, next to his decomposing corpse whore of a wife. No, she's not good enough to be called a whore; she was a goddamn pimp for that fucking kid of hers.

Saliva builds inside my mouth at the thought.

If it wasn't for Dex, I would have put her on ice and eaten the other eye as a cool treat on a hot day, such as today. But we still have him.

My cock hardens against my white jeans, but now is not the fucking time. Afterwards, we will celebrate.

"Let's get Izzie and head back. We have to do it tonight. You're ready." I say with absolute confidence.

His head shifts towards Izzie, admiring her from afar, just as he did when it all began. I watch as his chest rises slowly; she centers him, whether they know it or not. Moments pass before he returns his gaze upon me, and with one swift nod, Dex tells me he is ready.

Rising to my boot-clad feet, Dex's soft hand is still in mine as I gently tug on him to follow. Leaves crunch under our shoes with each step through the thick brush, looking back at Dex, "I get why. It's peaceful watching her. She is a fucking unicorn."

His eyes blink and his long lashes brush against his cheeks each time; his smile is boyish and contagious. Unknowingly, my lips join him, smirking.

I am turning into such a fucking pussy around him; a low chuckle leaves me at the thought.

"Izzie. Let's go." I shout at her as we enter the meadow.

Startled, her head flings towards us with wide eyes, "You scared the shit out of me, Liam!"

Waving my hand passively at her, I bark, "Now."

I know she's rolling her eyes at me; I don't need to see her face to tell. It's in her DNA. Izzie plasters on her fake smile and sarcastically responds, "As you wish, brother. I am nothing but your obeying sister." Which is followed by a curtsey.

Laying it on fucking thick today, isn't she?

Behind me, I feel Dex's arm move; turning around, I find him bowing in return, playing along with her dumbass games. My eyes widen in disbelief; now I have fucking two of them. Threading my fingers through my hair, I blow out a deep breath, wishing I had a joint with me.

"Not until I put these in water, Liam. Stop being such a fucking dick." My sister shouts while glaring at me with annoyance.

Rolling my eyes, I lean back against the countertop and wait. Dex looks at me; his lips are in a stiff grin, telling me that he is on her side. Traitor.

She takes her sweet fucking time filling the vase with fresh water, cutting the stems to an even height, then arranging them in some sort of organized chaos before putting them on the table. Placing her hands on her hips, she admires her work and prolongs my agony of waiting. Dex stands next to her, looking at the bright colors. He even leans in to smell them. Fucking traitor.

"We have a guy downstairs who not only is the worst kind of despicable and repulsive human being to be created, but who is also begging me to use his skull as a bowl and feast on his brain like spaghetti. Can we please hurry the fuck up?" My patience is quickly running thin. Once I have my mind set on something, I have to move now, or I get increasingly more agitated by each waking moment that passes.

Izzie reaches to touch Dex's arm but stops herself mid-air, "We should go. If we push too hard, he will only get more irritable, and we will never hear the end of it," she whispers truthfully to him. Teaching him my idiosyncrasies.

Turning around, Izzie's bare feet pad across the floor to the basement stairwell, Dex looks over at me, and I signal for him to go ahead.

Clapping my hands loudly, I shout into the air while stomping my feet, "Daddy dearest! We are coming for you!" A mischievous laugh follows. I want the last standing Ryan to be shitting himself right now. To be so fucking scared that he tries to stop breathing in an effort to kill himself before I can get to him, before Dex can fucking get to him.

Running down the wooden stairs, the dim lights are still shining, and the smell that invades my nostrils is nearly vomit-inducing. He is going to be a motherfucker to clean up later.

Izzie and Dex are standing against the cement wall. Their eyes watch me, waiting to see how this will all kick off.

I left some tools down here from the other night on the tables, out of reach from these vermin fucks. Walking to the edge, his feet are still securely wrapped down, and I take hold of my father's trusted scalpel. The same one he used on me repeatedly. The same one I then returned the favor to, with him. And now, it's Dex's turn to use it.

Placing the cold metal tool between his dad's toes, I glide it slowly from there all the way up the top of his foot, stopping just before his restraints. Looking up, the old man's lips are dry and peeling from dehydration, his eyes are drooping, and a pathetic whimper follows my assault.

"You deserve this. Everything that's coming your way, but it still won't be enough. Your wife was a pimp, and you fucking went along with it. Dex killed your daughter, then your wife, and next, you. And I killed your son." I taunt him; I like to play with my food first. Makes it more exciting. Holding my hand out, I wait for Dex to grab the scalpel, which happens almost immediately. As he takes it, I state with thrill and amusement, "Give me one more minute with him. Then he is all yours."

Walking to the head of the table, I stare down at this piece of shit. Taking the built-up saliva in my mouth, I release it and spit on him. It lands on his mouth. And the fucker is so desperate for water that he licks it off his lips almost instantly.

Absolutely no shame with this one. Not even an ounce of remorse or sadness when I mentioned his family being brutally murdered. He doesn't deserve to live. He doesn't deserve to breathe the same fucking air as us, my family.

My fists slam down on either side of his head; a monstrous and deep scream leaves me as my chest huffs vigorously. My vision tunnels; all I see is him, naked on the table and tied down with the silver duct tape. Helpless fucking loser.

"Liam, stop. You're scaring him!" Izzie shouts at me.

Her words are an echo in my ears, but don't penetrate my mind to comprehend.

Continuing, my fists bounce off the hard table; a throbbing sensation builds the harder I go. My words spit out like venom, "You never deserved him. I would kill you over and over again if I could. Then let him," pointing over to Dex while maintaining focus on the trash before me, "Cut and carve you as slow as he fucking wanted. Until his soul felt liberated. Free from the hell you had it buried in."

My heart is racing; I can't stop myself once I get like this.

I know he's scared, and I am sorry for it. But this is who I am. Take it or leave it.

This is me.

"Dex. You can't give your heart fully to us or anyone until you are no longer chained to the memory of your past."

DEX

His eyes are dark and as powerful as he is, it doesn't change the fact that his remark stings. Calling me out like that.

Fuck him. Pushing me when I don't know if I'm ready.

"He likes you. This is him helping. He just doesn't know how else to say or do it. And when he gets like this,

this is the nicest thing you will hear him say," Izzie murmurs to me.

She is taking care of me as much as I want to take care of her.

We watch him as Liam continues to look down at my dad. His body is tense; he's on edge and ready to attack. All he has to do is move his fist an inch over, and he would be pounding into my dad's face. To break his nose, for blood to be trickling down his face, and perhaps break a few of his teeth.

"I'll help bring him down after; don't worry, Dexy." She reassures me, and I think herself as well.

The veins on Liam's forearms are protruding, the tighter his fists clench, and the more he hits them against the table. My cock gets hard at the site.

Then a thought enters my mind.

His hands have taken so many lives. But they're saving mine. Just like mama and Jasper. My family is growing.

CHAPTER 20
DEX

I need to hurt him. Just like I need my heart to beat and for blood to course through my veins.

The same rush has arrived as it did with *her* and Karen. With my mom, I didn't feel anything. I think the shock of seeing her and dad strapped down, being within fingers reach, caught me off guard. Adrenaline kicked in, and I acted upon it. With dad, it's been building. The knowledge that he has been down here, helpless and alone. Vulnerable and unable to defend himself. I've relished it. Now they both know how it fucking felt to be me for years!

Seething, my fists clench by my side, and heavy breaths evade me. My eyes glare at the man who raised me; it's time. The cool metal scalpel is gripped tightly in my hand; moms was quick, but his, I'll ensure it is slow.

Walking next to the table, I take him in one last time. Shaking my head, he disgusts me, "Dex. I'm your father.

Remember? You don't have to do this, son." He pleads pathetically.

A loud slam follows, startling me; it's Liam, "He was never your son, you lying sack of shit!" His words are spoken between clenched teeth, angry and matter-of-factly.

"You must be his new mouthpiece. Did the psycho bitch dump you? She didn't want used trash, did she?" My dad's words penetrate me like knives to the chest. Mama will always fucking love me!

Lifting my hand, I react instantly. Taking the scalpel, I cut him without a second thought, just above the knee, where I make sure to get deep enough to cut his tendon. He's a thinner man, so it's easy to accomplish. A horrendous scream follows, but I block it out, just as I did with his daughter.

My vision is tunneling; it's only me, him, and this surgical tool.

The smell of his crimson blood makes my mouth water, and my body relaxes into the art I am about to create with him. With Karen, it was thousands of thin paper cuts and *her*; I skinned alive. With him, I shall decorate his skin with hate and despair, making his death just as slow and painful as the rest.

Moving to his feet, I cut the tape holding his ankles down, and one at a time, I lift them and slice each of his Achilles tendons. Dad's feet go limp in my hands, and more blood releases from him, this time coating my fingers. It's thick and warm, comforting. More screaming follows, I'm sure, but my ears block it out. Walking to the head of the table, Liam sets clear out of my way, not wanting to interrupt the process. I take the sharp tool and place it at the crease of his armpit, pressing hard. I move slowly, making sure dad feels every nerve tingling slice. And I don't stop there; no, I take the scalpel and decide I want to see his heart beat. Just as I have seen on Greys and make a clean cut down the center of his chest, his skin separates flawlessly and blood drains out of him. I drop the tool on the table and grip the two sections of skin; my fingers dig deep underneath and into this chest cavity for a better grip. Once satisfied, I put all my strength into pulling his skin further apart; the cracks and tears are music to my ears.

Clearly, I can see the whites of his ribs, the fullness of his pink lungs, and faintly hearing the throbbing of his beating heart. Closing my eyes, I take a deep breath in, basking in the glorious sight before me. My eyes are hooded and dazed, absolutely captivated by what I have done.

Allowing the skin to fall on either side of dad's torso, I grip the end of his rib into my hands and apply every ounce of pressure I can muster up to break them, one by one. He will experience some of the worst pain of his life with each break, and the thought has me smiling with glee.

Motherfucker deserves it.

Positioning myself next to him once again, it gives me better leverage as I make my way slowly through as many of his fucking ribs as I can. As the first one snaps, I throw the excess bone behind me without a care. Moving to the second one, I take it and taunt it in front of his face. Dad's eyes have welled with pain and discomfort, tears are beginning to flow freely, and drool is starting to fall down the side of his face.

With each break, I get closer to his heart, which is beating more rapidly as each second goes by. His body could be going into shock; on top of the blood loss, it's working overtime.

The bottom of his diaphragm and lungs are free from the confinement of his ribs. *I wonder what will happen if I give it a little squeeze?* I ask myself.

Unable to resist the temptation, I grip it in my hands and clench the diaphragm muscle as hard as I can. Dad's body convulses, as if the wind has been knocked out of him. His body automatically tries to inhale at the loss of oxygen, and I see his lungs desperately trying to expand. Squeezing down once more, his body tries to jolt forward but can't, thanks to the duct tape securing him down. Smiling, this feeling magnificent, being able to see how the body reacts under my touch—it's addictive. No wonder serial killers never stop. How could they?

My eyes shift briefly toward Liam as understanding floods my thoughts. Not that I cared, or that it bothered me, but it's only now that I fully get him and why he does it.

I allow myself just a moment to absorb this before bringing my attention back to dad.

My fascination with this diaphragm and lungs has moved on. I continue breaking away more of his ribs. The higher I get, the thicker they become. It's becoming nearly impossible to sever them myself. Just as I think that, a set of hands wrap around mine, Liam. He must have noticed the increased difficulty, and together we continue my objective. With every snap and crack, we get closer to exposing *the* sacred heart. The edges of his ribs are now jagged and sharp, and as I maneuver around them, I make sure to be careful not to cut myself. With the last piece we break, Liam lets go, allowing me to continue my work, my art. The corner of my eye catches him putting that final sharp piece of rib into his pants pocket, which makes me smile with curiosity.

Next thing you know, he will be using it as a skewer over the fire with some of his favorite meats and veggies.

Focus, Dex! I take my fist and pound it once against my head. Blood splatters around me as my fist connects, which only adds to the art before me.

Blowing out a deep sign, I'm back in the zone. The sight before me is splendid. Just what this fucker deserves. His blood loss is becoming excessive; slow and steady is no longer an option in his demise. I need to end him before his body ends it for us. I will not allow him to take another thing away from me—the free fucking will to kill him myself.

Reaching deep inside his crimson chest, more blood begins to pool inside the opening, making it more difficult to see where I need to go. Focusing myself, I allow my senses to take over completely. My eyes zone out as my hand moves under the jagged rib ends and his breastbone. The vibrations of his heart beating tickles my hand the closer I get. My knuckles brush along the powerful organ, which is responsible for pumping all this blood around us. I trace my fingers along it, and I am able to feel the veins and muscles along with an artery. As I play with it, I notice the beating becoming more shallow; I'm running out of time.

Wrapping my hand around his heart, I allow myself to feel his life beating a few more times before taking it.

Slowly at first, I squeeze the organ that is the size of my hand. Fascinating how it's the key to our survival, and yet I can hold it in my fist like this so effortlessly. The heart struggles with the mounting pressure that I am steadily applying. It's trying so hard to do something I'm no longer allowing—to beat, to pump blood, to live.

Squeezing my fingers harder, I feel like it's a balloon ready to pop.

Fuck. My eyes want to see. I need to witness it all, not just feel.

With one quick and fluid movement, my hand leaves his chest. And with it, his heart follows.

Blood coats it along with my hand as it trickles down my arm. Holding it before me brings me great satisfaction. Arteries are torn off, and its life is no more. And now, my troubled spirits are silenced.

CHAPTER 21
IZZIE

Liam is manic. His pupils are dilated from the high of watching Dex. As he pulled out his dad's heart and put it on display, I nearly vomited. I'm used to what Liam does, but I never stick around to watch it all. Once Dex is done admiring his work, he drops the heart to the concrete floor, where blood pools around. My eyes concentrate on it; I mean really focusing to see if I can catch an aftershock or a last beat coming from it. I'm sure I stand looking down on it for minutes without blinking, until hands grip my face, pulling me out of my trance.

Liam's lips crash against mine as he begins to devour me. I keep my eyes open and look into his, they are looking at me, but he isn't behind them. There is no spark or life glimmering from them; I need to bring him back.

Placing my hands on his chest, I push him away. He

stumbles backward, tripping on his own feet and nearly falling to the ground. I take the opportunity and reach for the scalpel. Clenching it in my hand, I take my brother's arm and make one quick and shallow cut. His head turns to look at me, and then what I did. Dropping the blade next to us, I then begin to coat my fingers with his beautiful red blood. Biting my lip, I have finally coaxed his attention to focus on me; his eyes are still dim, but he is coming back to me, a faint glint of him is trying to peek through.

Reaching for the straps of my dress, I slowly pull them down off my shoulders and allow my thin summer dress to follow. The coolness of the basement prickles my skin, and goosebumps rise in response.

The dress gets stopped at my hips. Taking my fingers, that are coated with Liam's blood, I drag them down my body. Starting between my breasts, they slowly make their way to my belly button, then my pelvis. My eyes glance to Liam; his cock is hard and pressing against his jeans, it's working.

Gripping the fabric, I shimmy it down to expose my aching pussy. As it falls to my feet, I step out of it and get closer to Liam. Gathering more of his blood from the cut I made, I take my fingers and place them between my legs and start coating my pussy with it while fingering myself. My nipples harden, and my hips grind against my hand. I keep eye contact with Liam, so he knows *he* is who does this to me.

I hear the sound of his buckle unlatching, followed

by the distinct sound of a zipper being pulled down. His hand then grabs ahold of my wrist and pulls my fingers out from inside of me. Bringing them to his lips, Liam places my fingers inside his mouth, and his tongue begins to clean them off. Low, throaty moans leave him as he devours a mixture of my cum and his blood. As he finishes with them, he slowly pulls them out, sucking to ensure he has retrieved every last drop.

Then, within a blink of an eye, he swiftly lifts me up by the armpits, and my legs instinctively wrap around his waist and my arms follow around his neck. My pussy uses his bare pelvis, working my clit against him, using him for my own pleasure, but he doesn't let that last long. We move, and without warning, my back is slammed against the foundation wall. At the same time, he impales his cock inside of me. My back arches into him, "Fuck, Liam. Come back to me, baby," I pant, moving my hands up his neck and into his hair. I pull it hard, causing his head to follow.

"You don't tell me what to do; I tell you, slut." His words are spoken with venom and defiance. *Just a little further, baby; you're almost home*, I think hopefully.

I let go of his locks, and at the same time, his hands cage me in on either side of my head. Liam's sharp teeth nip at my bottom lip, and with each bite, a familiar sting follows. We don't make love; we fuck. We fuck hard and fast, giving each other just what we need and desire.

His hips buck against mine faster; the friction inside of me sends me off into a frenzy. My sharp nails dig into

Liam's neck, scratching deep into his skin. Audible moans and whimper escape me as his cock works my sensitive spot. My body trembles as explosive currents race through me. In my sight, all I see are stars. My pussy grips Liam's cock before she begins to milk him; my orgasm has completely taken over my body. Sweat beads at my hairline, and my hips buck into him. Liam is quick to follow as he buries his head into the crook of my neck, nipping at my skin. I feel ropes of his warm cum mixing with mine. Our breathing turns into heavy panting as we both give into our release.

"You did this. Only you," I whisper breathlessly into his ear.

A muffled response follows, "Fucking liar. Dex could unravel you just like this if he wanted to."

He's not wrong.

As our moments slow, my eyes come back into focus, but my breathing is still heavy. The first thing I see is Dex standing in the same spot as before, but with his bloodied hand wrapped around his hard cock while his thumb circles his tip.

I look at him, speechless, not wanting to say anything that could spook him. Then a slight tilt of my lips makes my mouth smirk with pride.

Liam stays in me a while longer; none of us move from where we are until one of us does, Dex. Walking next to where we are still enthralled, Dex takes his blood-coated fingers and writes on the wall next to me in giant bloody letters,

NEED.

This time I gasp, not expecting this response at all from him. Liam returns from his haze to see what has caused such a reaction; his eyes search until they don't need to search anymore. His lips part and his eyes squint as he turns his face to Dex. My brother's lips move, but no words come out. I can feel his heartbeat pick up again.

He's absolutely in shock. I don't think he anticipated this day coming so soon. And now that it has, he's frozen like a guy who didn't just cum inside of me.

His cock pulls out, and my pussy misses him already. Our release drips down my leg, bringing me comfort. Liam places me on my feet, but my legs are like jello, unable to support my body as they drop me to the ground. My hands slap against the floor as I continue to catch my breath and bearings. On shaky knees, I crawl the foot to my dress that is still bunched on the floor where we left it and cuddle comfortably into it like a house pet and watch my boys.

DEX

I can't explain it.

Watching the two of them just now sent heat flowing through my body. I *need* him like she does. So with my cock hard and hanging out of my shorts, I tell him exactly that with blood and my finger against the wall.

At first I am taken aback by his response and body language; my mind tells me this is what rejection looks like. That he doesn't fucking want me.

I am so stupid.

Of course, he doesn't fucking want me.

My eyes well with tears as the adrenaline from taking a life dies down. All bravery is gone and only shame remains. Spinning on my heels, I face the wall and slam my head hard against it. Before I can get the second one in, a deep voice commands me to stop.

Liam.

My body is vibrating, scared, and worried.

"Are you sure?" he asks, unsure.

I nod my head in quick succession, knowing for absolute certainty this is exactly what I need. Tears trickle down my face out of fear and the unknown of what is to follow now that I have exposed myself.

We stand in silence for what feels like an eternity before Liam finally speaks again, "Then it's yours."

My lip quivers, still unable to look at him.

"I'll take it slow, beautiful boy, I promise." He reassures me.

Turning to face him, I give in and submit, allowing Liam to take full control over me and my body. I am absolutely terrified; my hands are shaking even, but I know deep inside of my soul this is the right thing.

Reaching his hand out, he holds my face gently. His

thumb traces my bottom lip, and I swear my heart is in my ears with how loud it is beating.

Breaking contact with me, my skin instantly misses his touch, but it's not long before it returns. First, he slides my pants down to my ankles, and I step out of them, he does the same with his. Both of us are bare and exposed, with nowhere to hide.

I swallow down the large lump in my throat as he steps back to me. His warm breath brushes against my skin. My hands clam up, sweating as they continue to tremble.

Liam places his head against mine and looks lovingly into my eyes. Our lashes brush against each other with each blink as he whispers, "At any point you need me to stop, tap repeatedly, and I will. That's your safe code, okay, baby?"

Our eyes remain locked in with one another when I take his hand into mine and write, *Okay*.

The second I finish the *Y*, his lips find mine; our kiss is gentle. He takes his time easing me into it. Parting my lips, I let his tongue in. His strong hands take my hips and pull me closer to him. Our cocks are touching, rubbing on one another, and the entire time all I can think of is, *I hope I don't cum yet*.

My ass flexes when Liam moves his hands further down my hips. Our tongues are still dancing. Unsure where to place my hands, I wrap my arms around his neck, like Izzie did, then tangle them in his soft hair. If we could get any closer to each other, we would. Our pull, our connection, is authentic and real.

His fingers trace my skin and start moving towards my backside. I'm nervous and excited. We grind into each other once more before I feel his finger circling my hole. Instinctively, I clench. Liam breaks our kiss but keeps his lips on me as he speaks. "I won't hurt you."

I relax back into him, allowing him to explore every inch of me if that's what it takes to have him.

His face moves, his lips brush against my skin, moving down my face, under my chin and onto my neck. An overwhelming sensation trickles over me as his lips continue to descend down my body. Liam removes his finger from my backside; both hands are spread wide, moving down my thighs. Lowering to his knees, he looks up at me with hunger in his eyes and my cock bobs before him. Opening his mouth, he takes me in, then grips my shaft, wrapping his fingers around me. My breath shakes as I exhale. Taking his tongue, he trails up the underside of my cock and teases me by lingering on my sensitive slit even longer. Circling my tip, he licks the precum that is leaking out of me. My toes curl and my eyes roll backwards.

"Don't you dare. I'm only getting started." Liam's voice rasps. His hands are still tightly gripping me as drool glistens down his chin.

Having to cum because it was forced is completely different than cumming because you need to, because it feels too fucking good to stop. I still don't have much control over that part of myself yet, but with Liam's help, I will continue to learn.

Rising to his feet, Liam takes me in once more before spinning me around and bending me over. Bracing myself against the wall with my hands, I look over my shoulder and watch him, waiting with anticipation for what is to come next. My balls tingle at the thought and desire rushing over me. His brows raise and confidence shines off him; his focus is on a single spot now. Stepping forward, his hand taunts me, softly rubbing against my backside. I feel his cock next rubbing against me; it only feeds my hunger further.

His thumb is first to penetrate me; I stiffen, unsure of what to do. Liam leans forward and softly says, "I need to stretch you, baby. It's ok."

Relaxing back into him, I let him work me. The longer he stays like this, the better it feels. Another finger is inserted, and I throw my head back onto his shoulder. At first it stings, but the longer he keeps it there, the less discomfort I feel.

"You're doing so fucking good, baby. I just need to do one more, okay?" His tone is soft and sweet; he is taking care of me, and I let him.

I give him one quick nod, and the third finger is inserted. My breath hitches and my body wants to tense, but I fight it; the more relaxed I stay, the easier it will be. At a slow pace, Liam starts moving his fingers. At first it feels strange, but the more he moves, the more I like it. My hips sway back into his hand with each gentle thrust into me. My cock is rock hard as a tremor of arousal flows through me.

Liam must sense it because, as quick as he was moving inside me, it stops and his fingers slide out. Raising my head off his shoulder, I place my forehead against the cool concrete wall. It feels so fucking good against my warm skin.

Behind me, I can hear Liam spitting a few times; my brow arches in confusion. From the corner of my eye I see his fingers dancing in the blood around us. Then I feel his tip slide between me and stop just as it reaches my entrance.

"Tap me to stop, and I will." He reassures me one last time before taking me.

His spit mixed with the warm blood, must be acting as lube as he gingerly starts to slide into me.

Liam stops after the first push in, allowing me to adjust and get comfortable. Once he can sense I am relaxed into him, he moves further. This happens several times before he is fully inside of me. The feeling may be new, but this, right here, is exactly how it should be, if that makes sense. His hand dances around my waist and rests on my pelvis, pulling my body into his warm hold.

"I'm going to start moving. It's okay if you cum, baby. Your first few times will be like this; nothing to be ashamed about," Liam reassures me with his deep, husky voice that is spewing with desire.

His body rocks against mine, his cock sliding against my walls, and my body clenches around him. Bringing my head off from against the wall, my cheek touches his. Pressing our faces together, we both feed off each other. Our panting is heavy and loud. His fingers spread against my skin, gripping me with the pads as his movements become more rapid. Sweat is dripping down my face; I feel so full. A tingling sensation starts building, from the tip of my toes to the base of my spine and into my chest.

Liam groans, "Give into me."

And I do.

Bringing one of his hands up, he cradles my cheek as I press harder against his. Loud moans erupt from me as cum shoots out of me. I squeeze his cock harder while it continues to work me, my eyes hood, and my breathing gets heavier. Shockwaves trickle throughout my body as my hips buck.

"Such a good fucking boy, coming for me like that. So fucking beautiful," Liam praises, which only encourages my release to continue. My toes spread wide as the tingling sensation continues. I never want this feeling to stop. This is more intense than the blowjob he gave me. I have never felt so good.

Electricity is igniting inside of me, almost like fireworks. I couldn't make a cohesive sentence right now if I even tried. His cock is working the most sensitive spot inside of me and I buck back, never wanting him to stop.

Focusing on my own pleasure, not because I am selfish, because this is so fucking new to me, I don't expect what I feel next. Liam cums inside of me, coating me. It's warm and addictive. Moving my hips, I work him more, needing him to keep going, joining me in this orgasm. I squeeze him tighter, and a loud moan follows from him. I place my hand on top of his, which is still holding my face.

My tongue sticks out of my mouth; the tip of his meets mine, and we allow them to dance while in our daze.

My body is shaking. My orgasm subsides as the final shots of cum leave me, decorating the wall in front of us. Liam's movements stop shortly after; his cock stays snug inside of me. I wish we would stay like this forever.

"Baby, you're going to get tired soon. Once the excitement wears off and your heart rate slows down," Liam warns and begins to slowly inch out of me.

I groan in protest, causing him to chuckle, "Don't worry, I'll be taking this ass as often as you let me."

With that, his cock slides completely out, and I miss it already. Another whimper of protest leaves me, and he follows it up with slapping my ass with his hand while still laughing. I turn around swiftly, crossing my arms and pretending I'm upset and flaring my nostrils. He knows I'm messing around because he cups my face and whispers, "Liar." Before crashing his lips into mine. The kiss is short but delicious. I wrap my arms around his body, holding him close. Liam rests his head against mine, just like earlier. My eyes start to feel heavy. He was right; I feel exhausted. Turning his head, he looks behind him to find Izzie fast asleep, curled into a ball in her dress.

Stepping back and out of my hold, Liam passes me

pants. I take them and put them on; he does the same with his, followed by our shoes. He scurries towards me and kisses me one last time before reaching down to pick up Izzie.

Liam leads the way and heads upstairs. Before I can follow, I take in the sight before me one last time. Both of them are dead. Unable to hurt another person directly or indirectly again.

"Dex," Liam shouts back. I hurry behind him, still feeling his release inside of me. I never want this feeling to leave me.

We make our way to his room, where he places Izzie on the bed. He follows with looking at me to see if I will join. I do.

Getting in next to Liam, I curl into him, resting my head on his chest. His fingers play with my hair as my eyes get heavy and start to close.

"We are your future, Dex." Is the last thing I hear from Izzie before I give into sleep.

EPILOGUE
DEX

It's been a couple days since the basement. And I regret nothing. In fact, I can't wait to do it again. Everything about our first time, my first time, was how it should have been. This has definitely opened me up to being even more intimate with Liam. I hope one day I could please him as much as he does me.

Izzie and Liam are still sleeping; it's mid-morning, and I've decided to surprise them with breakfast. Actually, just Izzie. Liam doesn't always eat first thing, and I am not fucking making him his preferred choice in meal. I'm not judging him; I fully support his choices, but I am not cooking it.

Mama has been gone for what feels like forever. As happy as I am here, I really miss her. I wish she was here after Liam and I had sex, so I could tell her all about it and I could see how proud she was of me. But that will have to wait for whenever they decide to come back.

Just as I reach for a banana, the back door goes flying open. Turning around to see who it is, my heart races nervously. Who has found us?

"No sex before Dex, he said. We don't have time, he said. JASPER! We had plenty of time; he's just eating a banana," Mama declares, standing in the kitchen. Her face is bright with excitement. Jasp walks in behind her, smiling, and then throws me a wink.

I hear them have sex often, but it still makes me cringe to think about it. But fuck do I miss them.

Mama rushes over to me, wrapping me in her arms. I drop the fruit and hold her tight back.

"We have so much to catch up on. But first, wake your friends. We got 'em!"

DEX
JOURNAL ENTRY

Liam's making me do this. Says writing will help with the voices. He scratches poetry on the walls but still kills and eats people. So I'm sure I should be taking medical advice from him...

I know you're reading this. I'm just being honest, babe. You're a little nutty, and I've lived in Sutton. You and Ms. O would get along well. Fuck. Anyway, your nuttiness is one of the things I like about you... and Izzie. Because, like mama and Jasper, you two make me feel fucking normal.

I'm not trying to be funny. Just honest.

And now that I think about it, Mr. H would love Izzie; he would be absolutely fascinated by her.

I wonder what came of those two? Oh well. A thought for another day.

Your bare body is lying next to me. Your eyes are resting along with your beautiful mind. Izzie is next to you, on the other side. Her long red lashes resting delicately on her cheek. I watch, with each breath taken, the shallow rise and fall of her chest. Mindlessly, my free hand is tracing the black ink on your back as I write this. I suppose this is more of an open letter to you.

You taught me pleasure isn't always pain. You freed me.

Not to take away from mama and Jasp. They were there for me at my lowest. Stayed with me without any questions and empowered me every chance they had. My family.

And bringing my bio dad here for closure is one of the greatest gifts I've been given. Next to yours, of course. All of it has been therapeutic.

The people I care for the most have never abandoned me. Never traded me or used me. And now my family has only grown.

I basically live here with you and Izzie now. After bio dad was handled, I felt calmness and peace. Change didn't impact me like it had previously. Only a few nights did it become too much, where you walked me back to the barn, back to mama.

Never did you or Izzie hold it against me. You both always knew healing would happen in my own time and process.

We are still testing the shared bed situation out. I'm proud of myself and how far I have come.

Mama is struggling a bit. But I go to the barn every day, and some nights mama and Jasp come here so she can cuddle me to sleep. I will always need them. And her comfort.

Sometimes I wonder if it bothers Izzie that we don't have a more intimate relationship, considering she is who brought us all together. She was my original obsession. I will watch her with you, Liam. I'm getting more comfortable getting off to it. But my body burns at even the thought of her or any female other than mama touching my skin. They say they aren't bothered and accept me for me, but it is always a lingering thought at the back of my mind.

I'm not going to overthink this. I will not let my past define me. My past brought me this far, and I'm determined to make it the rest of the way in life, on my own and with the help of the people who love me most.

My eyes are getting heavy. Perhaps I should sleep. My first journal entry. I hope I did this right?

Dex

PS. What the fuck did you ever do with that piece of rib you kept?

DEX
JOURNAL ENTRY

After visiting mama and Jasper, Izzie and I walked through the meadow, and I watched while she picked fresh wild flowers. Today she was wearing a light blue and white striped sundress with her woven sun hat. Freckles decorated her pale skin. She is stunning.

I've let her in more. We hold hands now and have been starting to hug.

And she and mama are getting along better. Progress is happening.

Baby steps, mind you, but still progress.

But today, as Izzie and I walked hand in hand back home, she stopped abruptly. I turned to look at her, confused as to why she wasn't moving with me anymore. Then, her tiny hands gripped my tee, and she tugged me down to almost meet her height. By then, I knew she was up to no good. Her face screamed mischief and defiance. In one fast movement, she inched up on her tiptoes and kissed my forehead. My heart stopped, my eyes widened, and my jaw dropped to the floor. I completely froze. Not a single breath left me for fuck, I don't know how long.

Her large green eyes stared back at me, waiting for me to react.

I was reacting. I was in fucking shock.

I was shocked that she did it. Shocked that it didn't hurt. Shocked that it felt nice. This has always terrified me—this intimate of an act with a female other than mama.

Once the shock wore off, my body relaxed, and a smirk formed on her face. This fucking girl knew exactly what she was doing and knows exactly what she is capable of.

Then she clasped my hand and dragged me behind her home. Like nothing happened.

I'm about to tell Liam. He is going to flip, and I hope fuck me with pride.

Until next time.

Dex

LIAM
JOURNAL ENTRY

I'm so fucking proud of you, baby.

When you read this, please don't cry. I'll think someone's hurt you, and I'll have to kill way too close to home. Beautiful boy, jailhouse isn't the look I'm going for.

I love you.

xx L

The End.

FINAL THOUGHTS

Your past does not have to define you.
You are not alone.
Your story does not end here; it's only the beginning.

xx
kins

About the Author

Kinsley is a Canadian, Dark Romance Author who dabbles in Taboo, Forbidden, Paranormal and is currently in her Erotic Horror Era. When she isn't plotting her next twisted book or watching true crime docs with her cats, you can find her working for the man. Reading. Or listening to Taylor Swift & Sleep Token.

Make sure you follow Kins on her socials and sign up for her newsletter to see what is coming next!

authorkinsleykincaid.com

Also by Kinsley Kincaid

FORBIDDEN

Let's Play

Within the Shadows

Lessons from the Depraved

Haunted by the Devil; The Devil's Society

Sinner; The Devil's Society

Homecoming; The Devil's Society

Unholy; The Devil's Society

Sweet SIN Slaughterhouse; The Devil's Society

Reckless; The Devil's Society - Coming Soon!

TABOO

Wrecked

Sutton Asylum

Sick Obsession

Dark Temptation: Part One

Ghost Dick; A Port Canyon Chronicle

Dark Temptation: Part Two

Lessons; An Extremely Fucking Taboo Extended Epilogue

Brothers Bond

Fuck Me, Daddy; A Port Canyon Chronicle - TBD

Taboo can be found via the authors' website.

eBooks & Signed Book Shop